Griff

Book 2 in Taryn's Camera

Rebecca Patrick-Howard

For Mom

Contents

Prologue

*B*one weary from traveling and still a little stiff

from the cold that clung to him like a virus, despite his evening in the tavern, he gratefully dropped down onto the bed and tugged at his boots. The bed gave a little moan under him and creaked when he moved, but the sheets and blanket smelled fresh. Someone had come up and built a fire when he was downstairs, and he was thankful. It was blazing now, licking at the pine logs and filling the room with a pleasant scent.

He'd spent almost eight hours in the coach today, traveling over ruts and washouts in the road until his teeth chattered from all the jarring. The last couple of hours were the worst, when the weather had turned first to sleet and then to snow. He'd never been so happy to see the lantern of the tavern ahead, beckoning the exhausted travelers with its light.

He'd only been planning on staying a night before moving on, but now, with his belly full of stew and whiskey, he thought he might spend one more. Nobody was waiting for him up ahead. Nobody missed him back home. What he had were the clothes on his back, a small bag, and a full purse. When he got set up in the new town, he'd find him a good wife, even if he had to send for one back east. Right now, though, he was on his own.

Shouldn't have eaten so much, he thought as he stretched out on the bed, the feather pillow bunching around his neck. Absently, he rubbed his stomach which was starting to gurgle. Or maybe he shouldn't have eaten so quickly. All he'd had in the coach was some dried venison and bread. He'd all but inhaled his first bowl of stew with its chunks of beef and potatoes.

Soon, the gurgle in his stomach turned to cramps, and he nearly didn't make it in time as he bent over the side of the bed and retched into the pot someone had thoughtfully pulled close. Mixed with the sour taste of whiskey, the contents of his recent supper left him with a force he'd never felt before.

When he at last felt like he was finished, he sat up on the edge of the bed and placed his head in his hands. His forehead, beaded with sweat, burned hot under his touch. Why was it so hot in here? The room spun before him, flickering in and out of darkness. How much had he had to drink? Three, four pulls on the bottle? He'd done much worse in the past without such bad results. Surely he wasn't coming down with something?

Another cramp seized him but this time he didn't make it to the pot and emptied what was left of his stomach onto the bed and floor. *Someone will have to clean that up,* he thought, but his mind had trouble focusing. Where was he again?

Gripping the small nightstand, he forced himself to stand. The spindly wooden table shook under his weight, rocking the oil lamp. The doorknob was only a few feet from him. If he could get out of the room, he could holler for help, maybe send for a doctor. Something just wasn't feeling right. But with each move he made, the door seemed to move farther and farther away, like one of those carnival mirrors. He dropped back down to the bed, fire running through his arms and legs.

Suddenly, a sound caught his ear. A knocking? No, it was a scratching. Faint at first, he almost didn't hear it for the ringing in his ears. It was coming from the wall, above his nightstand. "Damn mice," he muttered as he tried to stand again. The last of his energy left him, though, and he fell to the floor in a heap, his knees buckling under him like they were made of toothpicks.

"Help me," a hoarse voice cried from the spot where the scratching had been. "Help me!"

His last thought, before he saw total blackness, was, *My God, either I've lost my damn mind or someone's inside the wall!*

Chapter 1

I hope *it doesn't fall down around*

me, was the first thing Taryn thought as she stood looking at the old tavern and inn.

Her second thought was, *if it doesn't fall, I wonder if they'll let me move in?*

She'd worked in some pretty questionable places, but Griffith Tavern was standing on a wish and a prayer at this point. Oh, it was still beautiful with its wide porch, tall white columns, and hints of grandeur. And the flat Indiana farmland surrounding it made it more imposing. Without clumps of trees blocking it, the old inn and tavern stood like a sentry facing the two-lane highway. Tall and dramatic, it must have been a real beauty in its day.

That day had passed, however. Now, it was in shambles.

Taryn possessed more vision than a lot of people when it came to seeing the positive side to old buildings and houses. With enough money and time, she thought anything could be fixed. Termite damage? Not a deal breaker. Asbestos? Let's don some hazard suits and get to work! Structurally unsound? Dig deeper into the budget.

But this place? She wasn't so sure. Her optimism was waning by the second. Most of the glass was gone from the windows, probably knocked out by vandals from the looks of the graffiti and beer cans that littered the ground. Shards of glass plagued the dry, brown grass and reflected in the sunlight, twinkling like a million little diamonds. The front porch sagged in the middle and boards were missing in some places, allowing grass, weeds, and even the start of a small tree to push through. The roof had completely caved in on one side, leaving a gaping hole to expose that part of the house to the elements. As she took a few steps closer, the dead grass crunched under her feet. A flock of crows (or was it a murder of crows?) shot out of the hole and raced towards the sky, their calls filling the air with mockery.

Dark red bricks were crumbling, falling and stacking up like piles of leaves around the house. Anything wooden (shutters, window frames, etc.) had rotted away.

"Well, what do you think?" The energetic young man beside her positively beamed as he gazed upon the structure in admiration. "She's something else isn't she?"

Taryn estimated his age to be somewhere around twenty-five, but it was hard to tell with his full black beard and long dark hair hiding most of his face. His skin was brown and leathered from the sun, the T-shirt and khaki shorts he wore loose on his thin frame.

"It's um, really something else," Taryn agreed diplomatically. "But, goodness, it's gorgeous. Almost like something from the old south. I could see myself in a big dress, walking around this yard, handing out orders to everyone while I carried my parasol."

"Ha ha," Daniel laughed. "My girlfriend says the same thing. She loves this place."

Taryn's talent was in looking at the past and seeing what had once been. She had an eye for detail and a big imagination. Clients hired her to come in and paint structures that were in ruin, or simply needed a good renovation, and depict them in their primes. She might, for instance, be hired to paint a picture of a beautiful old mansion that was missing the whole second floor. In her

7

painting, however, the house would be intact and look as elegant as it had when it was young and full of promise. Sometimes clients hired her because they wanted to renovate a building and needed help with the visuals; they might not have a good idea of what it used to look like. Of course, some clients just wanted her paintings for sentimental reasons.

"So what are you planning on doing with it again?" Of course she already knew, thanks to the correspondence they'd shared, but now that she was looking at it in person she wanted to hear it again, just to be sure.

Clapping his hands together, the young man (Daniel was his name) grinned with eagerness. "When we formed Friends of Griffith Tavern last year my buddies and I just wanted to research the place, get a feel for it, you know? It's a big part of our history, you know, but everyone just ignores it. Then we decided to try and buy it. I mean, why not? She deserves to be rebuilt, kept up, and opened as a museum. You know she was in operation for almost ninety years?"

"But not always like this…" Taryn murmured. There were some modernizations done to it. She could see that from where she was standing.

"Oh, no," he agreed. "When it started out it was just a regular old clapboard boarding house. You could come in, grab some grub, spend the night, and then be on your way. That would've been in, oh, around 1820 I guess. Barns out back kept your horses fed and watered. Over the years, though, this grew up around it. It was a successful stagecoach stopover for a long time. That was its heyday."

"When did it close?"

Daniel thoughtfully rubbed his beard and chewed on his bottom lip. "Well, it officially closed as a tavern and inn in 1919. Railroad came through, new inns and taverns cropped out, original owners gone...You know how that goes. Things change. Somebody bought it and turned it into a little hotel after that but it was only open for about five years. For the rest of the time, it was used as a house. It's been empty for around thirty years now. You can see it's not in very good shape," he added hesitantly.

Yeah, no kidding, Taryn thought, *and it's a damn shame.* "Is it still in the same family?"

"Oh yeah. Not the ones who ran it originally, they didn't have any kids, but the ones who bought it in 1919 still have it in the family. Something like the great-grandkids or whatever. I can't remember the connection. But the new generation, they don't want it. I totally don't get that. Who wouldn't want *this*?"

"People lack imagination and ingenuity these days," Taryn agreed. "I wish someone would leave me an old house. Or, old inn as it may be. I'd live in it."

When Taryn's parents died, they'd left her the house. But it was a brick ranch house in a subdivision in Nashville. Not quite the same.

"Yeah, for real," Daniel agreed. "But these folks, they want to sell. That's when we decided to step in. We've applied for a grant and a couple of loans, and that would get us rolling. And that's why *you're* here. The first thing we have to do is get an architect to do some renderings. That's part of the grant stipulations. You're going to help bring it to life. We want to show everyone exactly what it used to look like and what it *will* look like when we're finished."

He clapped his hands again and let out a long breath of air like he'd been saving it all up just for this moment. He looked at her with so much admiration and hope that Taryn felt slightly embarrassed, blushing under his gaze. It was a good idea; Taryn knew, but she sensed there was more to it. "And then what?"

"Then we bring someone in to estimate the cost. We've found a historical preservation society willing to match the grant when we get it. And we WILL get it. After that, well, I guess we gotta start a Kickstarter campaign or something. That's how we raised most of the money to bring you in. We'll cross that bridge when we get there."

"But that's after you buy it outright, correct?"

Looking down at his feet, Daniel exhaled again. "Right. The grant will do that much. They've priced it at $175,000. Most of it is for the land because, you know, they say the house ought to just be condemned. But we can do it! We have to!"

Taryn could admire his enthusiasm, and she was glad to see someone doing their best to preserve a part of history. Still...

Buying it was one thing but this place needed extensive renovations. Those could cost half a million, or more. What would they do then? It wasn't her place to bring that up, though. She was just there to paint. "I'll do my part for you and that will at least be one thing out of the way."

"Awesome!" Daniel certainly was an animated little man. "We're so glad you came here. I actually borrowed money from my grandmother to help pay you. We know you're the best, and we're counting on you!"

No pressure, Taryn thought as she stared at the sad building. No pressure at all. She hoped the organization had more in their corner than her.

So what does it look like?" Matt, her childhood friend of more than twenty years, was on speaker phone as Taryn attempted to unpack her suitcase into the tiny dresser drawer. The closest hotel to the job site was more than half an hour away, but she'd found a B&B. She appreciated the owner's endeavor at providing original antique furniture to fit the style and age of the Victorian house, but there wasn't much room for storage.

"Like something out of a horror movie," she called in the general direction of the phone as she gave the drawer one final shove.

"Oh good," he chuckled. "Your kind of place."

She laughed back. "You know it! Of course, I completely want to move in. I already see myself on the porch, sipping on a mint julep and waiting for my beau to come up the road on his mighty steed."

"You want to live in every place you work at."

"Most of them, yeah," she agreed. She had a huge weakness for old houses.

Taryn made a habit of talking to him at least once a day by phone. With her parents gone and his dysfunctional without the "fun", they were the closest thing the other had to family. He lived in Florida, and her tiny apartment was in Nashville so they didn't see each other often, usually just over the holidays, but they talked every day and texted throughout it.

"Well, I met Daniel this morning," she proclaimed. Having given up on unpacking, she flopped down on the four poster mahogany bed and stared up at the ceiling, her phone resting on her stomach. "He's the president of the organization that hired me. Seems okay. Idealistic, but that's a good thing. It's going to take a lot of positive energy to get this place bought and renovated."

"Is it worth it?" Matt asked. She could tell from his voice that he was moving around too and had her on speakerphone. Sometimes they spoke to one another as though they were in the same room and not on the phone.

"It's *always* worth it," she replied. "Well, most of the time." She didn't have to mention Windwood Farm for him to know what she was talking about. Sometimes, it was better for the place just to be torn down and forgotten.

"So..." Matt left the word hanging in the air between them, a loaded question.

"I didn't feel anything. Sad at the condition of the place, but nothing unusual. Excited at its beauty and interested in learning more about it. Worried for the sake of the organization. But no vibes," she answered truthfully.

"Did you take any pictures?"

No, she hadn't. She knew she would but the thrill of photography had subdued her somewhat, especially considering what happened in Vidalia. The more distance she got from the situation, the more she let it get to her. The distance made her feel more vulnerable and the nightmares she'd always had since she was a child had grown more frequent.

"Not yet."

Matt groaned. "You've had two other jobs since then. Both of them turned out fine. You're going to be *okay*. But this is something you'll have to learn to deal with. You can't abandon Miss Dixie. Not after what you went through together."

Taryn's Nikon seemed to wink at her from the other side of the room, and she felt a little guilty for not taking her along for the ride earlier. It wasn't the camera's fault Taryn was seeing things she wouldn't normally be seeing. It wasn't the camera's fault ghosts, or something, appeared to her through its lens. She'd tried other cameras, and the same thing had happened. It was *her*. As the conduit, though, ignoring Miss Dixie felt like the only real way to avoid history repeating itself.

"I'll take her with me tomorrow," she relented. "I have to dive right into this one. They've got big plans for the place, and I'm apparently a great part of those. I can't waste any time."

"It will be okay, Taryn."

She sighed, kicked off her shoes, and sent them flying across the room. "Yeah, yeah. I know. I'm not afraid...exactly."

"It's okay if you are."

The only restaurant within a ten-minute drive to the B&B was a dairy bar called Jo's Frosty Freeze. It didn't have indoor seating and was the type of joint where you ordered your food at the window and then waited in your car, or leaning against it if you wanted to socialize. Most everything on the menu was fried, including the Oreos. Taryn was fine with that. Her stomach was apparently made of iron. Considering the amount of junk she stuffed in there, she figured she was built like a cockroach. The only real adverse reaction she'd ever had to anything she'd ingested was Pine Sol. Of course, that hadn't been by choice. Someone was, after all, trying to either kill her or seriously injure her at the time.

Jo's was a hopping place. As Taryn people-watched she saw middle-aged men with beer bellies, teenagers on skateboards, mothers with tired-looking children, and old women with hair nets and Cadillacs go to the window and order. It was early September so the air was still a little hot and sticky, and most people were enjoying ice cream cones and milkshakes. Taryn herself ordered a peanut butter shake, grilled cheese, and fried onion rings. She probably needed to go on a diet but could never find the time to start one. She didn't know any of the folks who were hanging around and waiting, but it felt like there was a community of sorts. Taryn enjoyed being a part of it, even peripherally. Middle-aged women chatted with one another; kids played together, the men stood to one side and smoked, a few rolling up their sleeves and pointing at grease stains or bandages. This was a gathering place; she figured that out right away, and she relished it.

While she waited, she replayed the rest of her conversation with Matt.

"So what is this place anyway?" he'd asked. "Was it a restaurant, an inn, a post office?"

Going into lecture mode, she'd responded in her best teacher voice. "Well, for the first fifty years it was in operation it was a stagecoach stop, or a weigh station for travelers. When the US Postal Service was created, a stipulation of the Act required the construction of roads to facilitate the mail movement. The stagecoach drivers operated on a relay system, with one traveling so many miles and then another taking over–at least on the longer routes. This let them move faster and was easier on the horses."

"Makes sense."

"Yeah," she nodded, although he couldn't see her. "The weigh stations offered this rest. Naturally, these new roads also opened up opportunities for travelers since it then became easier to travel from one point to another. Along with the new roads, an influx of travelers came the inns. After all, people had to have a place to stay for the night. They were like little Motel 6s, only with alcohol. My kind of place."

Matt laughed.

"The man who built it in 1838 ran it alone for a few years. Then he got married. He and his wife, together, more or less took it to the next level. They made the tavern part a little bigger, upgraded some things, and just made some general improvements. It was a pretty big deal around here."

Taryn could certainly understand why the Friends of Griffith Tavern wanted to purchase the building and restore it. There weren't many stagecoach inns left anymore, and it was a vital part of American history, not to mention local history. A real shame it had been left to deteriorate. In

Taryn's business, she found most people didn't recognize the true value of what they had until there was a threat of someone destroying it.

Driving back through town with her milkshake resting on the steering wheel, she surveyed her surroundings. The B&B was on Main Street, but the street was quiet this time of the afternoon. There were only a few shops open and no restaurants. The one diner was closed today. Mostly, the buildings wore lost, desperate facades with "For Rent" signs in their unwashed windows. When they built the interstate, it made bypassing many of these smaller communities easier, and the recent recession had left some of the towns in the Heartland virtual ghost towns. Few things made Taryn sadder than an empty, neglected house. She'd passed more empty houses and "For Sale" signs on her drive up from the Indianapolis airport than she'd ever seen in her life. For awhile, on the lonely two-lane highway, she'd seen one empty shell of a house after another—and many of the homes were new. She could imagine that at one time, not too long ago, they were filled with children's laughter. She could still imagine the smells of dinner cooking, the blare of the television drifting up the stairs as some silly comedy played.

They'd been *homes*. Now they were shells.

Sitting on the front porch in a swing at her B&B, watching the sun sink over the quiet street, Taryn flipped through her notes again. James Burke built the tavern in 1830. It remained in the Burke family until 1888. It sold at auction then to the Willoughby's. They kept it for thirty years until it changed hands again in 1919. It was still in that family.

Letting the swing rock her back and forth, she closed her eyes. With the swing's gentle rhythm lulling her into a soft sleep she imagined all the things the tavern must have seen over its time: the visitors, the excitement, the noise, and even the sadness. It would have been a revolving door for people coming and going, always alight with something new. The people in town would have used it for the food and drinks, too, and to gather news from the travelers about what was going on in other parts of the country. The building had seen more than some places ever would. Why did we believe newer was better? She was hardheaded when it came to that–a very good reason she'd majored in both art *and* historical preservation. Taryn had no head for business, but she appreciated the value of the past. And she could paint well.

Yes, letting Griffith Tavern deteriorate was awful. It deserved to be alive again, to feel the patter of footsteps on its floors, hear the sounds of laughter and music. The organization needed help. She'd do what she could.

It was late, but Taryn couldn't sleep. Instead, she'd drawn herself a nice bubble bath. She didn't have any actual bubble bath, but she always took hotel sample shampoos and soaps from her rooms when she traveled, and her suitcase was full of them. Emptying out five bottles had produced a nice froth.

She let the water run as hot as she could stand it, Andrew always told people if she couldn't boil a chicken in it then the water wasn't hot enough and let herself slide in. It was quiet. The other guests at the B&B were checking out as she was checking in. Nothing stirred; the only sounds were the soapy bubbles crinkling in the water.

I love my job; she thought, her mind feeling relaxed and a little mushy. I love being able to wake up every morning, feeling excited about going to work. I love being able to do something I enjoy.

She may have dozed a little. Her arms floated up to the top of the water and rested there, gently bobbing up and down. She knew she should get out, especially when the water turned tepid, but even the idea felt like too much effort.

Suddenly, a slight noise disturbed her reverie. It was a distinct creak from her bedroom, and it had her sitting up straight in the water. She cocked her ear towards the sound, straining to listen. Someone was walking around in the room. She knew that creak; she'd been making it all afternoon as she unpacked. The bathroom door was closed almost all the way to, but she was sure a shadow passed before it, and another creak in the floorboards confirmed it. She could feel the little hairs on the back of her neck stand at attention. Her arms chilled, goosebumps running up them.

The woman who owned the B&B? "Delphina, is that you?" she called.

With no answer in return, she quickly stood up and wrapped a towel around her.

Feeling naked and vulnerable, Taryn tiptoed to the door, her heart pounding so hard she could see the skin pumping through the towel. The creak came again; this time it sounded like it was close to her dresser. "Who's there?" She hoped her voice wasn't trembling. Despite the fact it sounded as though someone was obviously walking around on her floors, the air was eerily calm and quit. She couldn't detect any breathing.

The closest thing to her was a tall can of shaving cream, so she grabbed it and held it over her head, her arm shaking. With her other hand, she clutched at her towel.

Deciding to go at it all at once, like ripping off a Band-Aid, she flung open the bathroom door with her foot, ready to pounce on whoever might be lurking in the darkness.

The room was empty. She was sure she'd left the lamp on the dresser on. Still, even in the dimness she could tell nobody was in there. Her bedroom door was shut and locked from the inside.

"There's nobody here," she muttered. "I really must be going crazy."

But there was a feeling in the air that tugged at her, a feeling that she'd just missed someone. The air currents were still moving, still alive with electricity. She wasn't alone; she knew it. Whoever was there was gone, but there had been someone there.

Stomping over to the dresser, she switched on the bordello-style lamp. The light flickered for a moment, like it might not come on, and then the area was illuminated in a sea of gold. She was just about ready to turn around and head back to the bathroom to get her robe when the mirror on the dresser caught her eye. "Oh shit!" she yelped, stumbling backward and losing her grip on the towel.

Steam covered the large oval mirror. In its opaqueness, she couldn't make out her reflection or the rest of the room. In the very center, however, in large letters, the words "Help me" were written in a shaky hand. As she watched in dismay, they slowly faded until the glass was clear and she was staring back at herself, her mouth open in horror.

Chapter 2

On the early light of day, the poor tavern looked

even worse than it had in the pictures Daniel sent her. In fact, it looked worse than it had the day before. She was almost sure it was leaning to one side.

"We got an architect to come in and do a survey," Daniel had beamed. "It's structurally sound!"

Taryn had her doubts.

Two stories high, the front looked like a house. A large porch wrapped around the front and down one side and she could imagine chairs set out, welcoming visitors and offering relief on hot, stuffy days. Off the back there was a one story extension running at least fifty feet if she were to estimate. A peek in a back window (lots of cobwebs, but no spiders) showed her one large room with wood floors and a coal burning stove. More than likely, it was the restaurant section of the house and would have been filled with tables and chairs. Throughout the year, they might have even pushed some of those out and held parties and dances in the room. If she closed her eyes for a moment she could almost hear the stomping of feet on the floor, the walls vibrating with the sounds of fiddles and guitars as laughter trailed out the windows.

As for now, the only sound was an angry bee buzzing around her head. She must have disturbed it with her trespassing. Nature had taken over this place. Ivy completely blocked two of the doors and there were more wasps' nests than she cared to consider.

She was now itching to get inside and take pictures, despite her prior nervousness, but notwithstanding Daniel's zeal regarding the structure, the floors she could see didn't look too promising. Some were caved in. And then there was the worrisome bit leaning to one side.

Still, that didn't mean she couldn't window shop!

The porch held her weight and those windows revealed a beautiful staircase, two large front rooms, and an elaborate fireplace with what looked like marble mosaic—if the dust and grime on the glass weren't playing tricks on her eyes. A walk around one side of the house exposed too much poison ivy for her to get close enough to peek in. When she went on around, however, she managed to hoist herself to another window without any glass. Inside, she saw a set of smaller rooms that might have been a parlor and sitting room at one time. Overall, the front part of the building appeared sounder than the back.

Miss Dixie meant a lot to Taryn. Other than Matt, she was the only constant in Taryn's life. Her parents were gone but even when they'd been around they weren't exactly the warm, lovable folks you wanted to run to and confide in. They were nice people, but brittle; they were often lost in their little worlds and those worlds didn't even include each other most of the time. She could never imagine them being warm with one another, comforting each other, having sex...*not* that she frequently tried to imagine her parents' sex life or anything. Good God.

She'd met Matt when she was a child. Back then he'd just been a boy. She was too young to have racing hormones or develop any kind of crush on him. He'd had skinned knees, shaggy hair that hung down in his eyes, and always wore a jacket that was about four inches too short in the sleeves. He'd told her he was Indian and that his grandfather had been a chief. She'd noticed his slanted eyes and dark skin but had just thought he was Chinese.

Over the years their friendship changed and developed; it grew into something almost magical. She couldn't remember a life without Matt. It was comforting to have someone in her life she could turn to and ask, "Hey, remember when we were ten and..." or "When you were eighteen and I..."

Miss Dixie was almost the same. She was nearly a decade old, and Taryn had spent more on fixing her than it would've cost to buy a new one. Over the years, they'd gotten to know each other's quirks and intricate personalities. And Miss Dixie did have a personality; she had to be babied and taken care of as much as any person.

She knew most people would think she was crazy for naming her camera, but this one felt female and had a mind of her own sometimes. They'd been through a lot together, even before Windwood Farm. Although she was known for her paintings, she always shot with a camera first to get a feel for the place; that's how she learned about its nuances.

When Taryn walked back to her rental car to take Miss Dixie out, she felt *good*. It was a crisp morning, and the cars whizzing by on the highway behind her were close enough to make her feel protected but not uncomfortable. Even after what went down at Windwood Farm, she still preferred working alone. Now, however, she tried to be a little more practical about it. She *did* almost die, partly because of her own foolishness.

But Windwood Farm had felt "off" from the beginning; at least a little. She could be honest with herself about that now. Griffith Tavern was peaceful. Sad, sure, but the lingering energy was a good one. The house was already reaching out and grabbing at her with its tentacles, its energy engulfing her and slowly pulling her in the way all her favorite jobs did. But she didn't feel scared. She felt exhilarated.

But that didn't mean she'd forgotten about the night before. In fact, she'd barely slept. She'd kept both the lamp and television on the rest of the night and slept in snatches, regularly opening her eyes to peer around the room, convinced someone was watching her. She'd made it through the night, though, and in the clear light of day felt better. Perhaps it had only been her imagination. Perhaps they'd only looked like words...

Perhaps she was just trying to be rational and not completely freak herself out.

She wouldn't start her painting today. Today would be devoted to getting as much of the inn and tavern photographed as possible. She would start by walking around, taking general photographs of the outside. From there, she'd zoom in on the details and return to the things that caught her eyes. She wouldn't actually use any of the photographs she took, they were just for her own personal use, but the shooting of the place was an important aspect of what she did. Miss Dixie often worked as her second set of eyes and sometimes picked up on things that she couldn't see...in more ways than one.

Two jobs since Windwood Farm and not a single picture had come back bearing anything it shouldn't have. No ghosts, no ghostly furniture, and no scenes from the past. Maybe a couple of things that could be classified as "orbs" but they could just as likely been dust. Or bugs.

She was divided on how she felt about this. On one hand, she almost felt like she'd had enough excitement to last her a lifetime. On the other hand, she'd experienced a sense of achievement and peace for what she'd accomplished at Windwood, especially when it came to finally solving the mystery of the old house. She was uneasy about her "gift" (or whatever you wanted to call it) but that didn't mean she didn't want it.

But the night before...that was different. Something *had* been in her room. She was sure of it. And it wanted her to know it was there.

The day passed in a blur and Taryn was able to take more than two hundred photos of the tavern in all, even without venturing inside. It took several hours and would have been faster, had she not stopped and checked her LCD screen after every shot.

The pictures were all normal. The building might look like something out of a Dark Castle film, but it appeared to be harmless. Whatever had happened in her room may not have anything to do with the tavern. That was a charming thought, of course. A haunted B&B might draw tourists, but it didn't exactly make her excited to return. She wasn't necessarily afraid of ghosts, but she didn't relish the idea of something watching her while she slept.

When her phone started vibrating she knew it was time to pack it in and head back to the B&B. Matt always called her around suppertime and even though the sun was still out and the day had grown warm with the heat still hanging on, it was time to leave.

While she waited for the pictures to upload on her laptop back in her room, she ran herself a nice warm bubble bath and sank into it. She would talk to Matt while she soaked. This time, however, she left the door wide open and made sure both lamps in the bedroom were on.

As usual, he was cooking something. That's just what he did. Tonight it was homemade pizza: vegan, just because. He liked trying new things. She was glad she wasn't there to try it with him. Vegan cheese didn't sound like real cheese to her, no matter how much he insisted she wouldn't be able to tell the difference.

"You're ruining your body with some of the stuff you put in there," he chided.

"But I love Velveeta," she mock-whined.

"Don't you think there's something unnatural about cheese the supermarket doesn't have to refrigerate?"

"Well, what about the cheese in those fancy markets that they wrap in wax? Those aren't refrigerated, either," she pointed out.

"And they're also not irregular shades of yellow and orange," he retorted. "Or have the word 'spread' in them."

So the cheese conversation continued for the next half hour, and when she hung up she felt light and invigorated. Talking to Matt was one of her favorite things to do most nights, even when it involved inane things like Velveeta, cancer, and chemicals.

A glance at her laptop showed her the pictures were all successfully uploaded. Most of them were quite good, and she told herself this with pride. She was getting a little better with every job.

But they were all normal.

It wasn't the tavern then; it was the B&B. But who was there and why did they want her help? She was just barely able to take care of herself these days. How could she possibly help a ghost?

Chapter 3

*T*aryn had met with her clients in a variety of

settings—from swanky boardrooms with secretaries who brought coffee and sandwiches to penthouse suites in casinos. This was the first time, however, she'd met with one (or a group to be more accurate) in a storage unit.

"Sorry about the space," Daniel apologized. "Usually we meet at Moe's, the bar, but it doesn't open until 4:00 p.m. and I have to get to work. We rented this out to store some of our files and equipment in and it's the only real place we have to meet."

"I didn't think you'd want to meet in my dorm room." This came from a slightly overweight young man with shocking red hair who was busy rooting through his knapsack. "I'm a grad student and share a room with two other guys. They're a little noisy. I'm Joe, by the way."

The rest of the group nodded in agreement. They were a ragtag ensemble consisting of four women and three young men. Daniel appeared to be the oldest.

"So are most of you in college then?" This was also a first for her. Definitely the youngest crew she'd worked with.

"Yeah," a pert redhead in Army fatigues answered as she blew out a puff of smoke. She was sitting on a stack of boxes. "Some of us met in our historic preservation class. We're all different majors: art, history, econ…"

"We're a real organization, though, 501 (c) and everything. We have a board of directors," Daniel boasted hurriedly. "One of them is my old professor. He teaches historical landscaping at the university. Stand-up guy! You'll meet them eventually, but I wanted you to meet the real gang, first."

Man, where were these kids when I was in college, Taryn wondered.

A small blond with tight jeans and a lot of eyeliner was perched on a metal filing cabinet and studied Taryn with interest. "We're real glad you're here," she finally said. Her voice was smooth and silky and when she talked Taryn noticed the guys gave her their full attention. "I'm Willow, by the way. The group's official photographer and Daniel's fiancée. I know we probably don't look like the people you're used to dealing with, but we're totally serious about what we're doing."

"I can see that," Taryn conceded. "You've gone to a lot of work. Even getting the paperwork filed for the nonprofit part is a big deal. I'm not sure I understand what's going on, though. Have you already made a down payment on the tavern or what?"

Willow tucked a long strand of hair behind her ear and blew out a stream of air between her apple-red lips. "We have an option to purchase. It was good for ninety days. The good thing about it is that nobody can buy it out from under us before we get the funds..."

"And the bad thing?" Taryn sensed there was a "but" coming.

"It expires in less than a month, and we haven't secured the funds yet," Daniel explained. "And to answer the rest of your question, we're hoping to find the money. We've applied everywhere."

"Everywhere," the redhead echoed. "Joe here even wrote Oprah and Bill Gates."

The heavyset, redheaded young man nodded grimly. "It was worth a shot. Why not?"

Taryn resisted the urge to tell them finding the funds, even through grants, to buy the place and renovate it would be difficult under ordinary circumstances with all the time on their hands they needed. In that short amount of time, it would probably be nearly impossible. From the looks on their faces, though, she could tell most of them were feeling pessimistic about their remaining weeks, and she didn't want to encourage that. They needed to remain hopeful.

"We'd like to get the community involved," Daniel added. "Do some fundraisers, you know? We started a Kickstarter fund over the weekend. We've already raised almost $500. Joe here is our social media marketing expert. He's been on Twitter and Instagram and everything, just trying to get the word out."

"Just seems like nobody cares much about their own history anymore," a guy with shaggy auburn hair and a black Pearl Jam T-shirt said. "What's the *matter* with people? This tavern is one of the biggest things in the county and everyone's just letting it fall down around them."

Taryn smiled. "You guys are after my own heart. If I was rich, I'd already be poor because I would have spent all my money buying all the beautiful old buildings to fix them up."

The group smiled and a couple laughed.

"The couple that owns it? The guy is a descendent of one of the original owners, the one who bought it after the turn of the century. They're real sympathetic to us and want us to work it out, but they got hit hard by the recession. They need the cash," Joe explained. "Like, now. I think they've got a bunch of debts."

"I hear that," Taryn mumbled. "So if someone else comes along and tries to buy it after your option expires..."

"They'll have to sell to them. And that's already happened," Daniel muttered, studying his shoes. "A development company wants to buy the land, tear down the tavern, and build a shopping center there. It's a good location because in a couple of weeks they're going to start working on a new exit ramp off the interstate and then it will be prime real estate. We won't have a chance."

Taryn could see the disappointment and stress lining everyone's faces. She felt it, too. It seemed like there was always something in the way. "Then I guess we need to find money, huh?" she smiled. "A lot of it."

"Too bad the legend isn't real," Willow sighed. She stared off into the room, looking wistful.

"What legend?"

"There's a story that Permelia, the owner's wife, was really wealthy. He bought her from Boston. You know, a mail order bride?" Daniel let the question trail off as everyone nodded. "Well, supposedly she didn't have a family or anything but had inherited a ton of cash. Or gold. Whatever. Anyway, she brought it with her and hid it on the property. Nobody's ever found it."

"A buried treasure?" Taryn laughed. "That's awesome!"

"A few pieces of gold were found back in the eighties when they were doing some digging," Willow explained. "I can't remember what for. Anyway, it was in the ground. Probably just someone lost it somewhere along the way and it got buried in the dirt. They had metal detectors out for weeks. Never found anymore. Added fuel to the story, though."

"I bet," Taryn agreed. "Damn. Too bad that story *isn't* real. Gold would help. A lot."

Despite the good day she'd had, Taryn was feeling down. It was late and since most of the music channels had ceased playing actual music on television anymore she felt restless and annoyed. Music was her stress reliever but all her CDs were in the car and she was too lazy to go out and get them. Everyone was into Spotify and things like that these days but she didn't get those sites. Most online technology confused her, unless it had to do with photo editing. Even that had taken awhile for her to learn.

Fall was hard for Taryn. Her husband, Andrew, had died in October. They'd just been to a festival the day before. He'd eaten three caramel apples, the kind loaded with peanuts, chocolate, and Oreo shavings. She'd bought a handmade clock. The day felt so normal, no indication her world would come crashing down around her in less than 24 hours. Now she couldn't even smell caramel or listen to the song "Amazed' by Lonestar (they'd sung it at the top of their lungs on the drive home) without feeling panicked.

Funny how sometimes the good memories hurt worse than the bad ones.

She would feel much better once the air got colder, the skies darker and moodier, and fall was over. A lot of people hated the cold weather and snow it brought with it but she didn't mind it. It cleared out the sad memories for her, froze them.

Griffith Tavern was the first inn she'd worked at since Andrew died. Together, they'd worked at a handful over the years. There was one in South Carolina they had worked at and even stayed in together, but it wasn't a stagecoach inn. That one wasn't in bad shape; the owners wanted to renovate and restore it and needed some renderings for the architect, contractor, and decorator. It was a short, fast job but the inn itself was amazing and gave them the chance to stay near the beach and eat all the fresh seafood they could handle. On some nights they'd wander back to their room, stuffed and a little drunk, and would laugh and sing all the way there. Andrew couldn't carry a tune in a bucket and could get loud when he wasn't watching it so Taryn was constantly "shushing" him and giggling at the same time. They'd fall onto their canopied bed and roll around like children, priding themselves on being able to do something they loved, and doing it together.

She missed him.

Sitting alone in the middle of her bed, staring out the dark window into the night, Taryn cried a little.

She hated fall.

A short burst of rain left the ground moist and knocked down the temperature by a few degrees. The wet grass tickled Taryn's toes inside her sandals. It was easy enough to find a good, level spot to set up her easel and with several hours of daylight left she was hopeful she'd be able to get a lot done.

It had taken her forever to fall asleep the night before. No more spooky visitors but she was still on edge. And, sometimes, the depression hit her and kept her awake. She hadn't wasted her insomnia, though. She'd used it to study her photographs now she knew what she wanted to work on first–the porch–and had even made a few sketches. Her hands were still streaked with charcoal.

There was nothing like a good late-summer storm to leave everything feeling fresh and clean. Soft light filtered through the dark clouds still scattered in the sky and a hush fell over the tavern, giving it a wistful appearance.

It was a proud edifice and even with its broken windows and caved-in roof it still stood regally, unaware of its imperfections and brokenness. She could almost imagine it shouting out, "I don't care what you do to me! I'm not going down without a fight!" There would be no white flag for this one.

Taryn felt a sense of pride for the ragtag group and their confidence and nerve. She also felt a little bit of jealousy. She'd never had close friends like that, or even belonged to a group with a common cause. Her years at the university were spent either studying or working. She didn't join any clubs or organizations and didn't go out to listen to music or drink with the others (a fact that depressed her,

41

considering the amount of good live music Nashville boasted).

She was awkward around people her age and always felt like she was trying too hard with them—too hard to be funny, too hard to be likable, too hard to be interesting...to be noticed.

While she painted, she listened to music. Today it was Scott Miller; his version of "I'll Go to My Grave" got her every time. She'd seen him live several times and appreciated his wry sense of humor almost as much as his music. She'd also seen an image online of his old farmhouse. She'd love to paint it. He seemed like someone she might get along with.

Griffith Tavern was starting to come to life on her canvas, even in the black and white stage. She was still using charcoal, but the tavern was growing in front of her eyes as she filled in the holes and gaps. In her art classes, many of the other students had criticized her paintings for not having enough character or personality, for being too photographic—for not truly being "art," whatever *that* meant. In this job, however, it was expected and the very thing her clients appreciated about her work. She could get more creative and sometimes did on her own, but those paintings felt personal, private. She'd never let anyone actually *look* at them.

The longer she drew, the more inside her head she dove. She kept thinking about Daniel and his friends, her experiences at college and in high school. What started out as a small tinge of jealousy soon turned to the whispers of irritation and resentment. Why *hadn't* she made friends? Why hadn't she been able to find a close-knit group of people she could belong to? She didn't understand why she'd always felt so much like an outcast.

Driving her annoyance into her hands, she worked feverishly, shading and capturing the curve of the columns, the ancient brick, the stone steps.

She would be just fine on her own, she told herself. Just fine.

A ray of sunlight peeked through the clouds and hit a shard of glass still holding on in one of the upstairs windows. With the flash, the house seemed to wink at her, as if in agreement.

The rain was heavy and cold; the lightning fierce and strong. With each flash, it lit up the yard with a brilliant flare, illuminating the stables and gardens. The roar of thunder that followed was quick and bold; the storm was above them now and in its full glory.

She'd come outside barefoot, and the mud rose up between her toes and caught on the hem of her woolen dress. She was freezing, and it wasn't just from the rain and night air. She moved with determination, not giving in to the fear wanting to consume her. The tavern rose before her like a beacon, dark and foreboding. She walked towards it, keeping her eyes on the faint glow of light stemming from the upstairs window—her bedroom. When the sky was darkened, it was the only thing she could see.

Her breathing was heavy and labored, almost ragged. Her head pounded with a pain she'd never known, and it nearly blinded her. Only a few more steps and she'd be there, safe. Safe from what, she wasn't sure. She just knew she had to hurry.

When she reached the front porch, she stopped, shook the rain from her tangled hair, and looked down at herself as the lightning filled the sky again. From her dress ran rivers of dark water—not rain, but blood. It soaked into the ground and disappeared into the night. But her hands, oh her hands, they were covered. With the final burst of thunder, so loud the very ground shook in its quake, she screamed.

Taryn woke up; her covers pushed to the floor and her head pounding. She was drenched in cold sweat, her face and arms clammy with it. The television was still on, Tony Danza and Judith Light were bickering in the on-screen kitchen. Reaching for the remote, Taryn turned up the volume. She wouldn't be sleeping for the rest of the night.

Chapter 4

*T*he next several days passed without incident.

Over the summer, her doctor prescribed some Ambien to help with her sleep issues but she wasn't taking it regularly. Now, Taryn knew she might want to start. She'd always had trouble sleeping, and her nightmares felt worse than those she imagined most people had, but dreaming about the tavern had felt different. She had seen the rain, felt the wet grass under her feet, and even experienced the panic and confusion the woman in the dream was feeling. She couldn't think of that person as herself. They hadn't moved like her or thought like her—for Taryn, it was like watching a movie unfold through someone else's eyes.

Her two hospitalizations in Vidalia happened months ago, but sometimes she still felt like she was recovering. Being poisoned and knocked out, on two separate occasions, could do that to a person she reckoned. She wasn't feeling herself, though. She was still getting headaches almost every day and sometimes she felt a disturbing tingling in her left arm. Her doctor told her she might have suffered some nerve damage and given her more pills. One, however, made her lose the taste of soda, and she couldn't handle that so she didn't take them. A world without Coke and Sprite just didn't feel right.

She tried to think about the dream in a logical sense. What did it mean? What was it really about? Sometimes a horse wasn't sexual; sometimes a horse was just a horse. Maybe the tavern dream was about her loneliness, her frustration. Maybe it didn't have anything to do with the actual tavern at all.

Yet it had felt so real. She was there, experiencing the movements, but it didn't feel like her. She wasn't in control of her actions. She was still a little shaken by the fear she'd experienced, the horror. And she also felt...dirty somehow. Something wasn't right.

But, she had work to do. She had a job.

With her easel set up and her paints ready, she met Griffith Tavern with determination. Taryn painted with careful observation and skill. As she worked, she tried to consider the history of the place; how it might have felt to the early settlers who were moving westward to start new lives and find their fortune. Were they scared, excited, nervous? What did they plan on doing once they arrived at their destination? How many turned around and went back home when things got hard?

Taryn loved an adventure and liked to travel, but she wasn't sure she'd have been one of the early settlers trying to find her way out west. The stories she'd heard about the difficulties of traveling were enough to make her wary. Food shortages, native attacks, illnesses, accidents with the wagons and coaches...only the toughest were able to make it and even then it wasn't easy. Taryn, herself, was finding that the older she got, the more stars she required in her hotel.

The air around the tavern was thicker that day, more intense. As she painted in concentration, she got the distinct feeling the building was holding its breath, waiting. The sky was bright, not a cloud in it now, the grass thick from the rain. A light breeze cooled things off. But something wasn't right. With each brush stroke, she felt as though something was watching her, observing her, circling around her like a hawk. She turned around at one point, expecting to see Daniel or someone else coming up from behind her. Nobody was there.

The building in her painting was taking on its details in stride, emerging from the canvas a little at a time. Rather than looking as though she was creating it with her brushes, it looked like the image was already there and she was merely uncovering it, bringing it out from hiding with each stroke of the brush.

Standing back from the easel, she considered her work. It was darker than she'd intended. If a house could have a personality this, one would be proud. If it could have feelings, it would be lonely.

The air around her quaked, an almost audible sound. Then, when the warmth rushed over her and sent her hair flying, she could almost swear it had breathed a sigh of relief—a release of exaltation.

Hours later, Taryn stopped working and spread a patchwork quilt on the ground. She'd stopped at a grocery store and bought white bread, turkey, American cheese, and mayo to make sandwiches. There were bananas and apples to go along with them and a carton of Chips Ahoy. She told herself she'd only have a couple and not eat the entire bag like she did the last time she bought cookies, but she wasn't confident she could keep that promise.

When the white Buick turned off the highway and ambled towards her down the drive, she was curious, but not concerned. She assumed it must be one of the members of the organization. When the overweight man in khaki pants, white buttoned-down shirt, sports coat, and red tie emerged, however, she wondered if she was to be subjected to a talk by a Jehovah's Witness. He held a black notebook in his hand and had a Canon slung around his neck, though, so she figured she was safe from any religious spiel.

"Hello there," he called, walking towards her.

He must be sweltering, she thought to herself, and as if on cue he whipped out a handkerchief and started mopping at his neck. It wasn't that hot but the sun was bright and when it shone down without any protection from the clouds it got pretty warm in the field.

"Hey," she hollered back, rising to her feet and dusting the cookie crumbs off her shorts. "If you're trying to sell me something then you're at the wrong place. I'm broke."

The man smiled and ran his free hand through his thinning black hair. She pegged him to be around forty-five years old, although it was hard to tell with the extra weight. "No, no," he shook his head and pointed to his camera. "I'm just here to take some pictures and record some measurements. I'm from Longhorn and Reed."

The development company, she sighed. It seemed like she was always dealing with one no matter where she worked.

"Well," she tried to smile. "I won't bother you. I'm just here painting. I don't guess I'm in your way."

"No, no, you're fine. It's a nice drawing if I may say so." He walked the few feet until he was in front of it and shook his head in approval. Taryn folded her arms and waited while he inspected her brushes and palette. "You do good work."

"Thank you." Since he sounded sincere, she tried not to hold his profession against him.

"I know those kids who hired you want to make this place solid again, but the whole building's a wreck. Anyone could see that. Structural damage, rotted boards inside, termites, and even the brick's crumbling in a few places."

He used his notepad like a stick, pointing out weak spots from a distance while he talked. "The whole thing just needs to be torn down, in my opinion. The money it would take to fix it if it even can be fixed, is more than anyone around here is going to come up with."

Taryn bit her tongue but managed to flash him a quick smile out of southern politeness. "Well, they're optimistic it can be done. I've seen a lot places with more wear and tear than this rise from the ashes. So you never know."

Shooting her a condescending look, he shook his head. "When the exit ramp comes, this is going to be a highly developed area. We're looking at three restaurants, a Kohl's, a Target and that's just for starters. Give the people in this area a lot more options than what they have now. How far do you have to drive to get to any shopping around here? A Mexican restaurant? Half an hour? Trim that down to about ten minutes. Will totally revitalize the community."

Or evaporate it all together. And why can't the old and new coexist with one another? Taryn wondered. "Maybe. But you're also losing a valuable piece of the area's history in the name of progress."

"Sometimes that just can't be helped. Casualties and all. With so many of these small towns drying up, sometimes you have to make hard decisions for the good of the community."

He said it with a tone of regret, but she didn't buy it. He didn't look like he minded making those hard decisions. He'd barely looked at the tavern at all, except for when he was pointing out its flaws. He didn't see the same things she did, the same things she knew Daniel and the rest of them saw. "If we continue to demolish our past, how are we going to remember it?" she asked.

Wiping at his neck again with his handkerchief, he studied her drawing without meeting her eyes. "It's not such an important place when you think about it in the scheme of things. Just a stop on a route used more than a hundred years ago. Nothing noteworthy happened here, no vital part of history. It's just a small place. Of course, it's important to save the bigger places, and I donate to a lot of preservation causes. But this? In the scheme of things, it's insignificant."

Probably not to the people who owned it and made their lives here, Taryn thought as she watched him walk away, his camera held out in front of him. It wasn't insignificant at all.

With a click of her mouse, Taryn sent the last of her money to pay her monthly payment on her Capitol One credit card account. "Well," she announced aloud. "It was good to have it while it lasted." Now, her checking account wavered at exactly $21.56. She hoped that was enough to get her back and forth to the tavern for a few days until more money came in. Her previous client, a salt box job in Massachusetts, still owed her around $400. And the Griffith

Tavern folks would pay the remaining balance when she finished her job there. Most of that money would go to bills.

"Miss Dixie, our ship's gotta come in sooner or later, right?" But Miss Dixie just sat on the B&B room dresser and looked at her, stoic as always.

There wouldn't be any eating out this week, but she was ready for that and had gone to the grocery and come back with more sandwich meat, crackers, Hot Pockets, and Cokes. It would last her for a few days. She didn't have much of an appetite at the moment. Thankfully, the room had a microwave and a small refrigerator. The breakfast was pretty big, too, and she could always smuggle some bananas or muffins in her bag.

Feeling depressed, she fell back against her pillows and stared up at the popcorn ceiling. Had there ever been a time when she wasn't concerned about money? Now, it seemed to constantly be on her mind. How much did she have, how much did she need, and where was the next paycheck going to come from? She wasn't frivolous with cash by any means. The jean shorts and T-shirt she was wearing came from a secondhand store and cost her approximately $4. For both. The biggest payment she had, other than her rent, was her health insurance and she needed it. But it always felt like she was struggling.

She could get rid of her storage unit. That was costing her $75 a month and the money would be nice. But the idea of doing it made her ill. Andrew's stuff was in there and even though he died years ago and the pain wasn't as fresh, she still wasn't ready to face it. The last time she'd opened the unit his scent had hit her like a ton of bricks, washing over her in waves. The almost air-tight unit had sealed it in like chicken in a freezer bag. She'd closed the door as fast as she could and made it back to her car before she collapsed on the blacktop, crying a hideous amount of tears, her reason for going completely forgotten.

No, she'd keep it.

There had been nothing positive about his death, deaths rarely hold a silver lining, but at least his insurance policy was paid up and Taryn was the beneficiary. She sold the house, the boat, and his tools. Between that and the insurance payout, she'd managed to stay afloat for awhile. Then the recession came and a lot of people, especially nonprofits, suffered. Her work had also hurt. For nearly two years, she'd lived off the money from Andrew's death, taking odd jobs at rock-bottom rates to supplement her income when she could.

All of that was gone.

Work was picking back up, but it came in spurts.

Taryn was disappointed she hadn't bought something meaningful or even frivolous with the insurance money, something tangible she could look at and hold. Or at least taken a trip—something she knew Andrew would've appreciated. Instead, it all went to bills and daily living.

Even if she had gone on vacation or bought a new flat screen, she'd give up anything for the ability to go back in time and tell him not to get in the car.

Since she couldn't go out and eat, and she was tired of feeling sorry for herself, after a few hours Taryn found her way downstairs to the "library" of the B&B. The library basically consisted of two bookshelves stocked with self-help, romance, Chicken Soup for the Soul, and local history books. She'd already read everything she brought with her and she was willing to give anything a shot. Taryn loved to read, even the back of cereal boxes. A large hardback boasting the history of the area weighed at least five pounds, but she pulled it off the shelf and carried it out to the front porch.

So far, Delphina, the owner, was only accessible at breakfast time. Taryn wasn't sure where she retired to for the rest of the day but she appreciated the fact the proprietress didn't hover. She'd stayed at a few B&Bs where the owners wanted to follow her around, chat, and go out of their way to make her feel comfortable. While she did crave company from time to time, she felt awkward and uncomfortable when she was forced to socialize constantly. Sometimes B&Bs made her uncomfortable because she was constantly aware she was staying in someone else's home, and this made her nervous. Her studio apartment in Nashville was the size of a postage stamp and the stairwells and elevator smelled, but at least it was hers. In a B&B, she was always worried about oversleeping and missing a breakfast someone had put a lot of work into.

The front porch was wide and full of white wicker furniture, reminded her a little bit of "The Golden Girls'" living room. Taryn was still the only guest and had the place to herself. She chose a deep-seated chair, snuggled into the floral cushion, and started reading.

The book was fascinating, at least to her. She enjoyed learning about local history. The town was formally established in 1845, but settlers had been scattering there for several years before. When it became official, it boasted a general store, bank, blacksmith, stables, and the tavern. As an official stop on the stagecoach route, it wasn't long before other businesses sprung up, too. An old, weathered photo from 1880 showed a busy Main Street with shops and houses, some of which were still standing. Other boarding houses came and went, too, but Griffith Tavern was the first and most popular. It was also the largest and served as a type of community center for parties, gatherings, and events. This, of course, was what interested Taryn the most.

The proprietor, a James Burke, was the name she was already familiar with. He was married to Permelia Ramsey of Boston. The book didn't have any pictures of them, but several chapters mentioned balls, ice cream socials, and parties given by the couple. There were a number of pictures of the tavern and it had been a real beauty in its time, just like she'd figured.

When James passed away from a riding accident Permelia stayed on and ran the tavern until her death.

Taryn stopped reading at this point and closed her eyes. "Oh God, please don't tell me she murdered him," she whispered. "Please don't tell me things are going to get weird because I have to figure out how and make things right."

She didn't need to worry, though, because in the next paragraph the author talked about the accident that occurred on a farm outside of town. He'd apparently been with a few other men and a snake had spooked his horse, throwing him to the ground and then trampling him. There were at least four witnesses and he died almost immediately from what appeared to be a broken neck.

Sorry James, Taryn thought.

Nothing else was written about the tavern, except at the very end under "local legends." Taryn read on, fascinated:

Not long after the Reynolds family purchased the property in 1919 stories about buried treasure became popular. Millicent Reynolds found two gold coins in a flower bed. Two years later, while repairing the hardwood floors in a former upstairs guestroom, another gold coin was discovered by Stewart Reynolds. Little is known about Permelia (Ramsey) Burke but during her lifetime it was suspected that she was a wealthy woman and had brought a small fortune with her to Landon Crossing. Indeed, many improvements were made to the tavern during her reign. In 1981, a handful of gold coins were discovered outside when new electric poles were installed. However, it is assumed that the "buried treasure" story is merely that—a story. The tavern did go through droughts in which Permelia had to sell many belongings and even release employees, such as the stable manager and head cook, so it's doubtful she had a fortune buried away.

Knowing more about it, and the people who had lived there, made her sad. It always did. The tavern was once a vibrant, lively hub of excitement and activity for the town. Now it was basically being reduced to a pile of bricks in the middle of a field. And the buried treasure? Fascinating idea. She was disappointed to learn there was probably nothing to it.

Her room was chilly when she returned to it. The furnace by the window was warm to the touch; there wasn't a single reason why it should have been so cold. Taryn shrugged on her flannel robe and grabbed a pair of fleece socks from her dresser drawer. That helped a little.

Despite her misgivings about staying in a place that doubled as a private residence, she had to admit her room was cozy. The bed boasted a real quilt and patterned pillow cases, not the white ones a laundry service would just continue to bleach until the fell apart. The flatscreen television was new and modern and carried more than one hundred channels. The dresser and nightstand were antique and not massed-produced pressed-wood, over-priced items from a chain store. She also appreciated the hooked rugs and brocade curtains. She'd peeked into all the other rooms, and each one had a different look and design—no cookie cutter style here.

Standing in the middle of the floor and looking around, though, had her scratching her head. She was almost sure she'd left Miss Dixie on her bed. But, there she was, resting on the dresser. And her laptop, which had been closed and turned off when she went downstairs, was now open and booted up. She highly doubted Delphina would've come in and disturbed anything. The woman was about as quiet and reserved as a mouse, almost timid. She'd barely said a word to Taryn since she'd been there and was even shy about entering the room and cleaning.

The room was growing colder by the moment. The cold air didn't have a source she could find. Instead, it seemed to be coming from every direction. Taryn felt a full-body chill, from her toes to her scalp, and shuddered in its wake. She watched in fascination as she puffed out her breath and watched it hang in the air, a little cloud that slowly dissipated.

Something wasn't right.

Pulling the robe tighter, she walked over to Miss Dixie and picked her up. The camera felt like ice. She clutched it tightly in her hand, but it was so cold it burned her fingers. She hoped there wasn't anything wrong with the heat. It would be a pain in the ass to have to pack everything up and move to another room. With her teeth chattering and her hands shaking, she turned Miss Dixie on and aimed her camera first at the bed and then at the center of the room. Each flash cut through the cold air like a knife, leaving a ray of warmth in its wake. Taryn held out her hand, feeling the warm air dissolve as it was overtaken by the cold. This was no furnace problem.

"Hello?" she whispered, her voice unsteady. "Who's here? What do you want?"

The quietness was mocking, unsettling. Somewhere far away was the sound of something hitting the floor, a thud. Taryn jumped.

Shaking her head, she walked over to her laptop and inserted the memory card. Seconds later, her first picture popped up on the screen. Taryn gasped, not surprise at what she was seeing, but still taken aback. Where her four poster mahogany bed should've been there was an armoire. It was partly open, revealing a shirt sleeve. Her dresser was gone as well; a small youth-sized one replaced it. Several rag rugs were scattered on the floor. It was her bedroom, but it wasn't her time.

She stared at her screen as she dropped into the closest chair.

"Oh shit," she murmured, cradling her head in her hands. The coolness, her things moving on their own…it wasn't a quirk of the house or her landlady. She'd been summoned, in a sense. "Here we go again."

Chapter 5

*T*he dress was heavy on her and the fabric coarse

against her skin. It rustled stiffly when she walked and scratched at her calves as she climbed the staircase. Her feet were sore. She cursed the boots she wore, a size too big, and the way they rubbed blisters on her feet. Her stomach heaved with sharp pains.

It would never be the same.

From a string dangling around her neck, she produced a key and bent forward, placing it in the lock in the door at the top of the stairs. The room inside was cold and dark.

Using a match, she lit a lamp and watched as the room filled with a soft, warm glow. Outside, the wind howled, and the tree branches lashed against the windows as though they were clawing madly to get in.

Standing in front of her bureau now, she removed the pins from her hair. One by one she laid them in a little row. Her dark hair fell to her shoulders, thick and heavy as her dress. As the sounds of the wind and rain drummed through the house, she gazed at her reflection in the cracked mirror. Her hair was dull, her reflection pale. Her eyes had never looked duller.

"What have I done?" she murmured. A thin cry nearby shook her. She steadied herself on the bureau, ignoring the plea of the one who needed her. "What am I? What have I done?"

Taryn could still feel the dream, still felt inside it, even though she was conscious of being awake. She purposefully kept as still as possible, trying to remember every little detail. It was fading away quickly, already feeling more like déjà vu. She'd known the cold, heard the wind, felt the weight of the dress on her body. Felt the pain in her groin, in her stomach. It reminded her of horrible menstrual cramps. For a moment she'd known the other woman's unhappiness, her regret, and something else she couldn't put her finger on. But the reflection in the mirror wasn't Taryn at all.

It was impossible not to feel a sense of intrusion, an invasion of her privacy. But she wasn't scared, just curious. The house felt familiar, even though it wasn't a place she'd ever been in before. It wasn't the B&B, of that she was sure. Was it the tavern? Was the woman Permelia Burke? What could she want?

Taryn didn't have time to dwell on it because her alarm went off seconds later, and she needed to get up and get moving if she wanted to make it to breakfast.

She slipped on a bathrobe and a pair of socks and didn't bother running a brush through her hair or putting on any makeup as she headed down to the B&B's dining room. As the only guest, she could afford to be lazy. There was a time when she would've applied her makeup evenly, curled her hair, matched her shoes with her outfit. It wouldn't have mattered if there weren't many people there to see her; it just would've made her feel good.

Those days were gone.

Now, she felt more comfortable with her hair loose, allowing it to fall where it would, or in a ponytail. She still wore skirts and dresses, but they tended to be peasant ones that fell around her ankles or prairie skirts with cowboy boots. Her cheap sandals from Target were getting so old they flapped when she walked, but her toes had worn perfect grooves in them and she hated to see them go.

Delphina had already set up the breakfast bar with donuts, eggs, bacon, fresh fruit, and cereal. Cursing herself for not bringing a purse or something to stash some extra donuts in for later, Taryn loaded up her plate and sat down at the table. It was slightly awkward to sit at a table meant for ten people when you were by yourself, but at least she didn't have to make conversation with people she didn't know. Her dream had worn her out.

"I'm trying out a new recipe on the donuts," Delphina called from the kitchen. Her voice was brittle, and an onlooker might think her wiry seventy-five-year-old body frail, but Taryn had seen her gardening, cleaning, and even moving furniture around with the gusto of someone half her age. "I'm attempting to make yeast instead of cake."

"They're really good," Taryn replied, her mouth full of eggs. "I took three."

Delphina entered the dining room carrying a pitcher of orange juice and refilled Taryn's glass. "Honey, take them all. I'll bring you a plate you can take up to your room. If you don't eat them I will, and I don't need the sugar."

"Thank you," Taryn replied, grateful. She was still short on cash and could use all the extra help she could get in the food department.

"I don't have diabetes yet, but they say I have 'pre-diabetes,'" she continued sociably. It was the most she'd spoken. "I'm not sure what that means. It's not enough to give us actual diagnoses anymore? Now we have to diagnose it in advance? They seem to have a name for everything these days."

"I guess I know what you mean," Taryn chuckled. "My grandmother told her doctor once that unless it was going to kill her she didn't want to know what it was."

"Did you hear the storm last night?" Delphina moved around the room, straightening knickknacks and removing invisible dust with a rag. She was almost always cleaning something when Taryn saw her. Taryn had never seen her relax. "It rained something awful."

"I must have slept through it," Taryn answered.

"We don't get too many here at the end of summer. Mostly in the fall or early spring. Sometimes we get a doozy though. Good for the garden and grass," Delphina shrugged. "I just don't sleep like I used to."

"Neither do I," Taryn agreed. Had she just incorporated the sounds of the storm into her sleep and created a dream around it? She didn't think so, but it seemed possible and she couldn't rule it out.

"Are you getting a lot of work done up there at the tavern?"

Taryn nodded. "It's going well. It's pretty. I've only been there a few days, and I'm already dreaming about the place, the people who lived there. Occupational hazard I guess. It's not the first time. I get pretty involved. I hope the kids get their money so they can buy it. I'd hate to see it torn down."

"Oh, Lordy; me too honey. Me too. I can remember, back when I was a little girl, it was a house. They held meetings there for the Kiwanis. And my daddy went there for men's business," Delphina added primly. "The owner was mayor here for awhile,"

Taryn smiled at this reference to drinking. "Was it a nice place back then?"

"Oh, just beautiful. They'd get it all decorated for Christmas and at Halloween the owners would hand out the best candy. But then the money dried up and the poor old place has just been empty; goodness, I don't know how many years it's been now. People just don't have the money to keep a place like that up anymore and then it gets handed down to another generation who don't know what to do with it."

"It's the first stagecoach station I've been to," Taryn admitted. "I've been reading about it in your books here."

"My daddy could've told you some stories about it, my granddaddy, too. They would remember it when it was open as an inn. They used to have all sorts of parties there, weddings, and all kinds of guests." Delphina pulled out a chair and sat down across from Taryn. As the sunlight streamed in through one of the windows, it landed on top of her curly gray head and gave it an almost bluish tint. Her fingers tapped on the embroidered tablecloth, a set of rings sparkling. "My family has been here since the beginning of the town. This house here? My great grandparents built it. Been in the family ever since."

"It's a beautiful place. I love the tavern, too. It must have been something," Taryn prodded. "And run by a woman for a long time?"

"Oh yes. Mrs. Permelia. Shame about her husband passing when she was so young, and she not from here, but she ran that tavern well. She's buried on up the road here."

"I guess it wasn't easy running a business by yourself back in those days if you were a woman," Taryn mused. Then, realizing who she was talking to, she blushed. "It's not easy *now* either, or I'm guessing."

Delphina laughed merrily. "Oh, I can't say I wouldn't mind more help but I manage. My husband left almost ten years ago. Not a day goes by I don't miss him. Mostly in the evenings when it's quiet, and everyone's gone or in bed. I'd like someone to talk to. I reckon that's the way Mrs. Permelia felt, too, running that place alone. And you! You're by yourself, too, and a working girl!"

"I don't mind it most of the time, being alone, but you're right about the evenings. And the early mornings…" She let her voice trail off and ran her finger around the rim of her orange juice glass. "Sometimes I want to tell someone about my day or something interesting that happened, and then I remember I can't."

Delphina smiled, a soft one that lit up her face. "I'm sorry, dear, I didn't realize you'd lost someone too. I should have seen it on your face. We women, we usually know these things."

"My husband," Taryn conceded. "He's been on my mind a lot lately. The anniversary of his…passing…is coming up soon. In a few weeks. It gets a little harder this time of the year."

"It was sudden then?"

Taryn grimaced. "A car crash. It will be six years this year. Sometimes I still feel like he's out there, working, and just hasn't come home yet. We worked together and spent most of our time together. It's been hard to…adjust."

"My husband and I also worked together. It was his idea to open this place. This was my family's home and I've lived here all my life. Jerry, my husband, worked for the railroad. When he retired his pension didn't go far. I didn't work, you see, but we did alright. Then, with prices gone up on everything from food to gas, we needed the money. So any rooms in this house we thought we might make good innkeepers. We always liked having company!"

"I'm sorry, what happened to him?" Taryn asked. "Did he pass away?"

"Oh no," Delphina sighed. "Something that makes me look much more foolish than the average woman. Jerry left me to have his adventures. I shouldn't have been surprised when he left; for years he'd talked about going out west or down south. Maybe getting one of those big RVs and selling the place. He could talk a good talk! I could never see myself selling, though. It was my home. It was hard enough for me to go on vacation for a week and leave it behind. So, one day, he went off on his own adventure. With him gone it's hard but I manage." Delphina's face grew a little darker, her smile tighter. "I manage."

"It's all we can do, right?"

Despite her full breakfast, and the fruit and donuts she'd hoarded, Taryn was still hungry and stopped at the Frosty Freeze on the way to the tavern. A turkey and cheese sandwich would keep in her cooler and a Coke on ice would get her motor running. She was dragging more and more. She tried to tell herself she was still recovering from being poisoned, maybe more than once, and a concussion but part of her was still worried. Shouldn't she be feeling a lot better by now? The exhaustion never really went away and the headaches were getting worse, if anything; they were not getting better.

The little building was crowded when she pulled up. Half a dozen people wandered around, waiting for their orders. A small group of teenagers sat on the red picnic table, looking at one boy's smartphone and laughing. They ignored her.

Taryn smiled to herself. Some things didn't change. Technology might get better, teenagers might feel wiser, but the lure of milkshakes and hamburgers would always be strong.

After she had placed her order, Taryn walked back to her car and perched on the hood. She replied to a text from Matt (just asking her how her morning was going) and checked her email. After that, there wasn't anything to do but wait. She didn't have a smartphone and could only perform basic functions on hers. The glare made it too bright to read. Still, it was a nice, warm day, and the beat of the sun on her bare arms and legs was soothing. The lull of conversation around her, everyone seemed to know each other, was comforting. She could almost take a nap.

"Don't fall asleep there." The low male voice made her open her eyes and she raised her hand to shield the sun to get a better look. The man stood near her, close but not hovering, and smiled. He was tall with dark blond hair and a slight stubble of a beard laced with red. He wore dusty jeans, a blue stained T-shirt, and cowboy boots caked with mud (or something). He appeared to be in his early thirties and was attractive, if a little battered.

Because he seemed friendly and harmless enough, she smiled back. "I *could* go to sleep. That sun's about to do me in. And it's still early."

Taking that as a welcome, he moved forward and leaned against her car. "It's a nice one today. The rain last night cleared the air. Supposed to rain some more the next few days. I came up here for lunch, take some back with me."

"That's more or less what I'm doing, too. You work nearby?"

"I work up at Jenson Stables. You know it?"

Taryn shook her head. "I'm not from around here. I'm just in town for business."

"Ah, well, I manage the horses up there. Show horses. Some riding lessons, too. A few boarders. Mostly show, though. You ride?"

"Not for a long time," she answered. In fact, she couldn't remember the last time she'd been on a horse. She liked them well enough, though.

"How long you here for? Maybe I could take you riding sometime," he offered with a smile.

Taryn could feel the warning signs, signs he was hitting on her. They prickled at her skin and made her tense up. She immediately went into defense mode. ""Well, I'm pretty busy. Lots of work to do."

Before she could say anything more, her order was called and she had to go to the window. When she walked back to her car, though, he was still leaning against it.

"I didn't mean to make you nervous or anything," he said, this time a little shyly. "I'm not real good in these situations. If you decide you'd like to ride, though, here's my business card. And I'm Jamie, by the way. I promise I won't kidnap you, come on too strong, or send you a friend request until you get to know me more."

She took it and tried to smile as she thanked him. She felt like a moron. "How can I resist an offer like that?"

"I have a sister. If she was out of town traveling on her own and a dude asked her out, I'd warn her to stay away—far away. You can't be too careful these days. And now I've gone and done it myself. I have references, though," he laughed. "See the woman standing over there by the silver Cadillac?"

The woman in question appeared to be in her late seventies and was delicately nipping at a twist cone. Taryn acknowledged her.

"She was my high school art teacher. I've lived here all my life."

"How do I know you're not just picking out some random stranger and pulling my leg?" Taryn teased.

"Hey, Mrs. Meade!" Jamie shouted. The older woman turned, looked at him, and smiled.

"Hello Jamie!" she called back.

Jamie looked back at Taryn with a smug grin.

"Okay, okay," she laughed. "I'll *think* about it..."

On the drive to the tavern, she replayed the scene. There wasn't any reason she should've been standoffish to him. He seemed okay, and he was nice-looking. As a woman traveling alone, and without a wedding ring, she got hit on a lot. At least this time the guy was easy on the eyes and close to her age. She felt a little ashamed of herself for not talking to him more. It wasn't his fault, after all, that she was awkward.

She wasn't a stranger to dating since Andrew's death. In fact, it was her past experiences with dating that made her hesitant to pursue anything. About five months after Andrew died Taryn found herself going out on a date. A client set her up with a man whose fiancée had recently called off their wedding. Taryn knew it was a bad idea the moment she agreed to it. She was lonely, though, and everyone kept telling her to "move on"–and that Andrew would *want* her to see other people and be happy.

The date was average at best: dinner and a movie. She couldn't even remember what they'd seen. Afterward, they'd gone for a walk around a lake. He was charming in a simple kind of way and had complimented Taryn a lot over the course of the evening. Somewhere between skipping rocks and talking about music, she found herself making out with him. She had no idea how it happened, but they ended up on the ground, her jeans pushed down around her ankles. It was nothing but sex, and not even very good sex when it came right down to it, and it was over before she could catch her breath. In fact, during the whole time she found herself singing Kelly Willis' version of "Don't Come the Cowboy with me, Sonny Jim" the whole time–especially the part about counting cracks on the wall. As she'd stared at the sky and watched the stars she couldn't help but think, *this is the same lake Andrew and I had a picnic at a year ago.*

She didn't see the guy, Craig, again.

That didn't stop her from seeing other people, though.

She'd repeated the same scenario at least three more times.

Finally, one night as she was sitting in a rocking chair in her living room she received a text message from the latest man. It was full of sexual innuendo—some of it badly misspelled. She figured it was supposed to be sexy and turn her on. Instead, it made her angry.

She knew she meant nothing to these men. But worse, they meant nothing to *her*. She'd turned something she'd once thought sacred and magic into something base and crude.

"It's normal," her therapist had told her. "Many people react to the loss of a loved one in this way. It's as if you're proving you're alive by engaging in intimacy. And, because you know you're going to feel guilty afterward, you might also be punishing yourself for the accident."

Taryn hadn't seen the therapist again.

There were no more dates for Taryn after that, though. Still, she made the mistake of telling Matt what was going on, and instead of being supportive or at least listening to her, he'd lectured her.

She'd cut him off, too.

Once completely alone, she'd gone on a tear through her house, removing pictures, bagging up clothes, and pushing most of the furniture that reminded her of Andrew into one room. After several months, when even that hadn't helped, she'd put it in storage and found a new place to live.

Taryn had been single for almost five years without even a casual date. She and Matt made up. But she still couldn't trust herself. Maybe she was punishing herself. Maybe all of her wires were just crossed.

Maybe she didn't know how she felt anymore.

Her turkey sandwich all but forgotten, she attacked her canvas with aggression. The lighting was good, despite the threat of rain and the storm clouds looming overhead, and Griffith Tavern rose before her, bleak and naked in the field. It was more imposing today and Taryn used this to her advantage. She was feeling dark and impassive herself. The paintbrush was light in her hand as she mixed colors, blended on her palette, and painted lines in firm, aggressive strokes.

I'm going to tell a story, she announced to herself, *about a tavern that was owned and run by a woman. It's a male building, but it was female command that kept it going. That's what I'm going to paint.*

In most aspects of her life, she felt awkward, uneasy with herself. In college, her clothes had been too bright, too colorful, for the young professionals already walking around in their black sweaters and business suits. Even in a town known for its country music she'd been embarrassed about her love of George Strait, Dwight Yoakam, and Patty Loveless, especially considering everyone she knew were all into grunge and alternative. Nobody had understood her friendship with Matt.

But when she painted...that's when she felt like herself. Even in high school art class when she hadn't been very good and only her art teacher encouraged her, she'd been happy.

Stoically, the tavern observed her in much the same manner she scrutinized it. Her sundress (she was down to her dresses since she couldn't afford to do laundry at the moment) clung to her legs and ants scuttled over her feet. Her hair hung limply to her shoulders, matted in some places where the sweat gathered and dried. Thick, gooey mud was smeared across one cheek. A strap fell to her elbow, revealing the hint of a beige bra underneath.

She didn't notice any of this.

Angry at herself even more now for not taking the nice man, *Jamie*, up on his offer and fed up with being so broke, she painted on.

Finally, when the sun started sliding in behind the clouds and she realized she'd need more linseed oil to continue, she stopped. Her canvas stared back at her, a quarter of the way completed. The real tavern waited in expectation, anticipating her next move.

Her energy had vanished, though, and she was drained. It was looking like rain, too. She couldn't do anymore today.

After loading the car with the canvas and paints before it came a downpour, she grabbed Miss Dixie and began walking around the tavern. She was finished painting, but she wasn't finished with her day. There were still things she wanted to do, needed to do. She might work on the painting back in her room and she could use more images.

The clicking of the camera was comforting to her and as soothing as any tonic or pills she'd ever taken. She aimed Miss Dixie at the windows, the porch, the field in the back (which used to be full of trees, she was told), and the piles of bricks that had once belonged to the building but were now in heaps around the yard. She'd taken more than fifty pictures before she realized it and the first few drops of rain had her scurrying back to the car.

The tavern faded into the gray sheet of rain behind her, forlorn and unmoving. Its windows were its eyes, however, and even without looking back she could feel them on her as the muddy water from the puddles sloshed against the side of the car.

Taryn could see the image from across the room. She'd put her memory card in her laptop and stepped into the bathroom while they were uploading. When she returned, the picture that glimmered at her had her taking a step back and slamming her shoulder into the wall behind her. Even ten feet away, it called to her and grabbed. She could feel the room start to spin, her vision growing fuzzy, the blood rushing and pounding in her head. She steadied herself on the bathroom doorframe; sure she'd pass out, and yet she couldn't take her eyes off it.

It was the last one she'd taken, a shot of the back of the tavern. You could clearly see the gaping hole in the roof, the fragmented glass hanging on in the windows, and the poison ivy imposing itself on the brick. All of that was expected. But what looked at her wasn't.

"Oh geeze," Taryn moaned, sinking to her feet.

Standing in the dusty, grimy glass on the second floor, was a well-defined figure of a woman. It wasn't a trick of the light, double exposure, or any other normal photo justification. From her distance, Taryn could still make out her dark hair, upturned nose, deep russet dress, and pale fingers pressing on the remainder of the glass. She knew the face as well; it was the same one reflected back at her in the mirror of her dream.

The woman, Permelia she reckoned, gazed out with sunken eyes and a frown. Her hair was groomed, her dress form-fitting and fashionable. Still, there was a look of desperation about her that made her appear on edge, frazzled—as though she might break at any moment. The way she seemed to be pushing on the glass gave the appearance of someone trapped, someone who was shut off from the outside world and wanted desperately to be a part of it again.

And she was looking right at Taryn, although she hadn't felt a thing when she was taking the picture. Her dark eyes bore into the camera, through the lens, and straight into Taryn. The idea of being watched, observed, without her knowledge made her shake. How often were these presences aware of us, she wondered, while we had no idea they were even there?

Crossing her arms over her chest, Taryn tried to get it together. She couldn't concentrate with Permelia's image staring at her look that. She felt exposed. Was there nowhere she could go to get away from this? She actually kind of liked the idea of having a link to the past she loved, but this time it was going a little far: she'd dreamed about Permelia, felt a presence in her room, and now she was watching her.

Why her? Why Taryn? Had she done something, said something, *thought* something that encouraged this? Was she doing something wrong or very right?

Could she go through this again?

Chapter 6

*S*he must want something, right?" Taryn paced back

and forth, the room growing smaller by the minute. "I'm
seeing this for a reason. Aren't I?"

"I would think so," Matt answered carefully.

"Shit."

"And nothing's happened since Kentucky? Nothing at
all?"

"Not a damn thing," she replied.

They were both quiet, contemplative. Taryn stopped pacing and looked at her bed. It had been made but was now rumpled from where she'd stretched out on it. Suddenly, she felt lonely. She didn't know why, but she had the craziest urge to hug Matt. Not just a quick one, either, but a long one. A snuggle. At this moment, she just wanted to find a cozy couch where the two of them could sit down together so she could bury her head in his chest and close for eyes for awhile.

"Matt?"

"Yep?"

"Never mind," she sighed. What was the point? If she asked him to fly up now, he would. But just because she was lonely and feeling out of sorts didn't mean he should disrupt his life and enter her chaos.

"You should go back, try to take more pictures. But be careful," he cautioned. "I can research the area, see if there're any shops where you might pick up some supplies."

"I feel safe enough," she replied honestly. And she did. "I don't know that sage and a wand are going to help me because I don't think she wants to hurt me. Or that anyone does."

Not this time, neither one of them had to say.

"If you need me, I'll come up there," Matt asserted with surprising sternness. "I have vacation time."

"Oh, I'm sure. The last time you took a vacation was two years ago."

"I can get someone to cover me here."

Taryn grinned at the thought. Matt hated to leave his office. Being away made him nervous, as he was sure the whole place would fall apart without him. "I'm okay. You don't have to come up here. But maybe when this job is over I'll come down there for a little bit."

"That's a good idea! I've been meaning to try out some new restaurants and, well, I don't mind eating alone and I do it a lot but I like having someone with me when I try a new place. And then there's the lighthouse they just got restored, you'll like it a lot, and the pavilion at the beach has live music every weekend until the end of October–"

She let Matt continue making his plans while she laid back on the bed, tired. Matt loved playing tour guide when she was there, and most of the time she enjoyed it. But at the moment the thought making her the most excited was crawling into the bed in his guestroom, shutting the black-out curtains, and falling asleep under the hum of his window unit air conditioner. She thought if she could do that, she might just sleep for a week.

"I'll let you know when this job wraps up," she promised before she hung up. Of course, she had no idea where the money would come from to go down there but something usually came up. She'd drive if she had to and just pull over and nap at rest areas. She'd done that before.

Daniel sat in the grass at Taryn's feet, his long legs stretched out. Today he was wearing shorts that showed off his muscular, but ashen, legs. He had a long look on his normally cheerful face as he fiddled with a blade of grass and twirled it around. Taryn felt sorry for him.

"So they didn't give you a reason at all?" She hoped she sounded compassionate and disappointed for him. The truth was, though, she wasn't too surprised. Grants of the caliber they were applying for had a lot of competition.

"Not a thing," he mumbled. "Just a standard form letter."

"I'm sorry, Daniel." This she said with conviction, because she *was* sorry. "Surely there's something else…"

"Yeah, maybe," he shrugged. "If we had more time to look. But we don't. No way we're going to find the money in a couple of weeks. I think we just have to face the fact it's going to be bought, torn down, and nobody even cares."

Taryn knew when it was time to work and time to talk and Daniel obviously needed to talk. Although she'd been making steady progress all afternoon, she laid down her brush and knelt on the ground next to him.

"I care. And, you know, others will. They may not know it before it's too late, but they'll remember it and talk about it."

"It's not the same though," he sighed. "The building will be gone."

"I know what you mean. In my job, I fall in love with a new place almost every day. Well, it feels like it anyway," she smiled. "Unfortunately, most of them get demolished. It breaks my heart every time. I've tried to learn new ways of coping with it, but that doesn't mean I don't care."

"I think there's something special about the tavern," Daniel stated. "I know you see a lot of these things and it might just look like another old building, but it feels like there's something here. I can't put my finger on it. I just feel drawn to it. It's hard to explain. Sometimes I feel like maybe I was there in another life or something. I believe in that stuff."

Taryn came close to telling him about the pictures she'd taken the day before. She had a hunch he'd appreciate them and they might improve his afternoon. But she wasn't ready yet. The only people who'd seen them was Matt and Rob, the owner of New Age Gifts and More in Lexington. She didn't know if she could show to them anyone else at the moment. They were for her, of that she was sure, and she didn't know what the "rules" were for sharing them.

"Oh, I'm very interested in it, too. I was just reading about the history of it. It's pretty fascinating. I didn't know much about the stagecoach stations until I got here," she said instead.

"Not too much written about this one, but I've talked to some of the older people here in town and recorded them for an oral history project. Some of them still remember when it was a tavern. Not the original one, of course, but they still remember. And others remember their grandparents talking about it. Kind of unusual to have a woman running it all those years," he added.

"Permelia," Taryn affirmed, remembering the shadowy figure in her pictures. "She must have done a good job to keep it going."

"I have a little bit of a crush on her," Daniel admitted as he rose to his feet. "She's kind of my historical girlfriend. You know, like a book girlfriend? Some of the stories I heard...well, she was interesting."

"How so?"

"Most people say she was quiet. Liked to sit out on the front porch and read in the evenings. I dig that. But also that she ran to anyone who was hurt or sick and fixed them right up. Never complained. That she was a serious businesswoman and even the men around here respected her. But that she gave the best parties and was always ready to dance and laugh and keep the beer flowing."

Taryn laughed. "Sounds like my kind of woman!"

"Mine too," Daniel smiled.

They shared a moment of silence, both staring at the tavern and thinking their own thoughts, until finally Daniel broke the quietness by fishing for his car keys. "I guess I need to go back home. I have a paper due. I'm taking this course in museum studies this summer. Once it's finished I just need to wrap up my dissertation and I'm done."

"What's your dissertation on?" Taryn asked. She remembered her college days, how eager she'd been to get out. Looking back, she wished she'd tried harder to enjoy it more while she was there.

"You know the Shakers, the religious group?"

Taryn nodded.

"Whether or not they achieved religious experience through, well, actual religion or through psychological manipulation brought on by segregation, fatigue, and personal affliction."

"Damn," Taryn whistled. "And what do you think?"

Daniel smiled and scratched at his beard. "I think if you get me up at the crack of dawn every day, make me work hard, separate me from my wife and kids, tell me I'm not allowed to have fun or do any of the things I enjoy anymore and then throw me in a building at night and say it's okay to scream and shout–I'm probably going to feel some kind of release."

"Good point. I always liked the Shakers, though," Taryn mused. "Very organized souls with their chairs hanging on their walls and minimalism."

"And they did give us the modern day broom," Daniel added with a laugh.

Taryn spent the rest of the afternoon in a painting frenzy, catching up on the lost time she'd spent talking to Daniel. She liked Daniel and missed his company; she felt a nice, easy kinship with him and was sorry about his grant. He was still young, naïve, and hopeful. He'd lose some of that along the way, especially with his field, but she hoped he held onto those qualities as long as he could. He'd need them; the *field* needed them.

Taryn took a walk at the end of the day, after she'd wrapped everything up and stored it in her car. The traffic on the road behind her was light now and only a few cars lumbered by.

The early evening light hit the bricks, causing the tavern to light up against the darkening sky and giving them a rosy glow. It was a lonely spot, despite its close proximity to town and its position on the road.

One thing was for sure—when they put in the new interstate exit things would pick up around here traffic-wise. *Especially*, she thought grimly, *if they threw in a few big box stores and a multiplex*. Not that she, herself, was above a little retail therapy but it seemed unfair that in order to have great shopping they had to destroy all the fields and farmlands. Taryn would've been perfectly content to go back to even the way things were when she was a kid and there were still big department stores on Main Street. Sure, you might have to go to a few different places to find what you wanted and her grandmother had grumbled more than once about having to drive into Nashville for a dress, but there was adventure in it. Now, everyone just seemed to move through these big stores with dead eyes, never stopping to talk to each other or really look around. It took the joy out of shopping.

Matt would say there had never been any joy in shopping in the first place. Then again, he was still trying to squeeze into his high school letter jacket at the age of thirty–

not because he had any nostalgia about those years (they'd been torturous for him, band geek and all) but because he hated to shop.

On the last trip back to her car, something made her stop and turn around. It was just the faint whisper of a breeze, nothing that should have been disturbing, but the deliberateness tugged at her and made the tiny hairs on the back of her neck stand up. She had the strongest feeling someone was watching her and that someone was not looking at her from the road, but from the supposedly deserted house. Thinking about the picture from the day before, she hesitated, not sure she wanted to pursue the matter.

Nothing was there. The house was quiet, the windows empty. Yet, something hovered; a viscidness that surrounded her and made it hard to catch her breath. It pushed down on her from above, gently but with great pressure. Taryn closed her eyes and, focusing on her breathing, tried to dispel the invisible suit of armor that enveloped her. Little by little, it eased up until the air felt normal again.

She turned back to the car and started towards it but she'd barely taken two steps when the breezes stirred again, nipping at her neck and fingers.

Ever so gently, Taryn laid her paints down on the ground and, moving in slow motion, turned to face the building. At first it looked the same as before, nothing appeared to have been moved or manipulated in any way. But there, standing in a downstairs window, was the unmistakable shadowy outline of a woman and she was staring straight at Taryn.

Taryn jumped a little but didn't look away. The energy radiating from the house was hot and palpable as Permelia's eyes bore into her. She couldn't turn her head or ignore what she was seeing, despite the fear that crept down her spine and reached into her heart.

For a brief moment, the two solitary women watched one another with equal curiosity. Neither the figure nor Taryn moved; time itself seemed to stop for just an instant as the currents between them sparked. Taryn could feel a bond of sorts that felt as real and solid as the ground underneath her feet. She couldn't make out any distinctive facial features but had the impression of long black hair falling around her shoulders and a dark colored dress. She was neither smiling nor frowning, but possessed a sharp look of concentration, as though she was unable to find the words she was seeking. Taryn could still hear the faint hum of cars behind her but they felt a million miles away, in another place and time. Even the old tavern glimmered dimly, wavering in the chasm the two women formed. For a moment it was intact again, whole, and then it was in shambles. As confused by the events as Taryn, it wasn't sure which version of itself it should be.

Taryn was much calmer than she thought she'd ever be, faced with a situation such as this one. Right before the figure shimmered away, shimmering was the only way Taryn would be able to describe it to Matt later, she lifted her right hand in a kind of wave and Taryn knew she was directing it at her. The bond dissipated and the force threw Taryn to the ground, the wind knocked out of her. Before scrambling to her feet she thought she'd heard a cry of pain, but she might have been imagining it.

Chapter 7

*S*o what did you do?" Matt asked with genuine

curiosity.

"I waved back," Taryn answered. "You know, it felt rude not to."

"I don't know that I would've stuck around once I saw her."

Taryn had trouble explaining how she'd felt compelled to stay, that she probably couldn't have moved even if she'd wanted to. And that, although she'd been scared, she was also curious. A huge part of her was almost disappointed when their link was interrupted.

Delphina'd taken pity on Taryn when she'd seen her sitting outside on the porch with her computer. She'd fixed her a plate of cheese, crackers, and fruit: supper.

"After all, I was on her property…"

"In light of the situation I'd say waving back was probably the appropriate thing to do," Matt agreed. His voice was muffled against the phone.

"You're getting undressed, aren't you?" Taryn asked, accusingly. "What, are you planning on taking me in the shower with you?"

"Well, not today," he laughed with uncharacteristic flirtation. "But maybe another time. It's just blistering hot here today and I was sweating. I needed to cool off."

"Do you think this is just a random haunting?" Another guest had checked in while she was out but she hadn't seen them yet. Their car was in the driveway so she figured she'd see them at breakfast. She'd been at the B&B for almost two weeks and it was the first guest the business had had, other than her, since her first night. She wondered how Delphina managed.

"What do you mean?"

Chewing on the bottom of her lip, a bad habit that often let her sore and raw, she tried to articulate her thoughts. "Do you think she wants something out of me or am I just seeing things?"

"It sounds to me like you think there's a mystery there," he teased. "And that maybe you should call Fred, Daphne, and the gang to come and investigate."

"Hey, I thought I *was* Daphne!"

"I don't think so, I always saw you as more of a Velma type," he mused.

Faking outrage she snorted. "Are you saying I'm nerdy and fat?"

"No, I'm saying you're smart and have big breasts."

With the first real laugh she'd had in awhile she wished him a good evening and hung up. With any luck, she'd have some emails from future job prospects and wouldn't have to worry about money so much.

Unfortunately, there weren't any emails, and no clients were sniffing out her services, but when she checked her bank account she did discover her last check had been deposited. She wasn't rich, but she had cash flow again.

"That's it," she announced as she smacked her laptop shut. "I'm going out to eat. This calls for something processed and fattening."

Taryn knew when to hold back and when to celebrate.

Later that night, in bed, Taryn wasn't so sure the fries, cheeseburger, apple pie, and milkshake were a good idea. Now she was running back and forth to the bathroom more times than she'd like.

Almost an hour had passed since her last bathroom trip and she'd been lulled into a false sense of security. She'd even been dozing a little when the cramps seized her again, sending her scrambling out of bed to make a mad dash back to the toilet. She dozed again while she sat there in the dark, her arms and head resting on the sink beside her. With bleary eyes she washed her hands, dried them on the soft hand towel, and trudged back out the door, hoping this would be the last trip for the night.

When she crossed over the doorway, however, she stopped cold in her tracks. The silhouette of a woman, quite similar to the one who had stood in the window of Griffith Tavern earlier that day, now stood in her own window and stared out at the lawn. Although her back was to Taryn, she could still see the long dark hair. The air around them was already changing and Taryn shivered as she took a step backwards. Where could she go? What was she supposed to do? This close to her, it was obvious the woman was tall and thin, taller than Taryn anyway, and even stately.

"Jesus!" Taryn finally shouted, falling into her door. It might have taken her a moment to react, but she wasn't so used to seeing weird crap at this point that she was unaffected at the sight of ghosts in her bedroom.

At the sound of Taryn's voice, the woman turned partly around and cocked her head slightly to the left with a small smile. She had a startling beautiful face, almost angelic with its fine features and porcelain complexion. A faint glow emanated from her, as if someone was standing behind her with a flashlight. She nodded her head, an acknowledgement, and then, swept away by a breeze, she vanished.

On shaky legs, Taryn staggered across the room and sat down on the edge of her bed. She fumbled with the switch as she flipped her lamp on. She didn't think she'd be sleeping in the dark tonight. There was still a strong current in the air, almost like static. Her hair was still standing on end.

"Okay," she said aloud, a little surprised at the power in her voice. She felt like she might pass out. "You obviously want something from me. But I don't think I can help you unless you stop scaring the living daylights out of me and are a little clearer with what you're after."

Maybe it was her imagination, but the air almost certainly rippled in response.

"I'm not good at this, Permelia." At the sound of her name, the bedside lamp flickered off. In darkness, Taryn tightened her fists and waited for something extraordinary to happen. She prepared herself for a hurricane of activity, for the face of a ghost to appear inches away from her own, for her room to start spinning...

All was quiet.

Leaning forward, she flicked the lamp back on again. Like hell she was sitting there in the dark. "I don't know what you think, but I'm not a medium, I don't have some kind of magical sight. Well, okay," Taryn conceded. "I do have a *little* bit of something, but I really don't think I'm what you need."

Now that she was talking, she was surprised at just how easy it was to converse with the ghost. It wasn't so different than talking to herself really.

The air was still now, though; the room empty. Whatever had been there was gone; Taryn was sure of it.

Still a little stunned, she got up from the bed and grabbed her phone. Even though it was in the middle of the night, she sent Matt a text:

Ghost visited me tonight. Why? Nothing to do with B&B.

She'd no sooner laid back down and closed her eyes when her phone went off with a few notes from "Me and Bobby McGee."

"Hey," she answered. "You still up?"

"Working on something," he lied. His voice sounded sleepy. "You had a visitor?"

She quickly filled him in on what happened, still shocked at the intensity of her appearance. Despite what had occurred at Windwood Farm, she'd never really interacted with a spirit before. At least, not since she was a child and that memory grew dimmer every day.

"It doesn't have anything to do with where you're staying," he said, putting reason to her thoughts. "It's *you*. She's attached herself to *you*."

"So she's followed me home like a stray puppy? Well that's a scary thought. Does she think I can magically fix whatever it is she needs?"

"Maybe," he replied thoughtfully. "I need to think about it. It might be something else. Is there something you could do for her? Something nobody else could?"

"I don't think so. She's dead."

"Well, there are three things going on here then. Either she wants you to do something for her, something she can't do because she's dead, or she wants to be known. I've heard of that happening, too."

"Yeah, well, what's the third thing?"

"Uh, she's just crazy and wants attention?"

"Great," Taryn quipped. "That's just what I need."

"Well, maybe she thinks you're a kindred spirit. You know, two working girls trying to make it alone in the world," he suggested.

"I can just see the sitcom now," Taryn muttered.

"I was serious."

"So was I."

Matt was silent.

"What *could* she want after all these years?" Taryn asked at last. Why show up now?

"Maybe she's afraid someone's going to tear down her house," he suggested. "And she wants you to stop it. God knows if it was you and your house you'd probably haunt someone until they threw themselves at the dozer."

Taryn didn't see Delphina at breakfast. Warm French toast with berry compote, scrambled eggs, and biscuits were waiting for her and she stuffed a few muffins into her day pack, despite the fact her financial forecast had a much better outlook this morning. You could never be too prepared.

After breakfast she changed into her work clothes for the day, a pair of capris and a sleeveless top since it was still warm in the afternoons, and started out to her car with her canvas and paints. At the edge of the porch, Delphina knelt in the grass on a blanket and busied herself with her roses. She looked up and smiled when Taryn walked down the steps. "Thought I'd get a head start on these while it was cool this morning. I've been meaning to cut them back," she explained.

"They're beautiful," Taryn conceded, admiring the flashes of color and velvety petals wrapping around the railings. "I've never been good at raising flowers. Had a garden a couple of times, but flowers aren't my thing."

"I treat my roses the same way I would my children if I had any," Delphina laughed. "I spoil them. Did you enjoy your breakfast?"

"Yes, I did. And I was meaning to ask you, and I don't want this to sound funny or anything, but it's about the Tavern..."

"Sure, hon, what it is? Oh, damn it!" A thorn pierced through her finger and a trail of blood began trickling down Delphina's wrist and dripped onto her jean shorts. She immediately placed her finger in her mouth and sucked on the injury, wincing at the pain.

"Can I get you anything? Some water?" The patch of blood on the old woman's shorts spread out like a small fan.

"No, no, I'll be fine. Just forgot my gloves this morning. It was foolish," she sighed, rocking back on her heels.

"I can get them for you," Taryn offered. "Just point me in the right direction."

"No," with a wave of her hand Delphina pooh-poohed the idea. "They're all the way in the basement and I won't have my guests playing maid to me. It was time for me to take a break anyway."

"I don't mind," Taryn tried again.

"Nonsense. I should keep them up here in the shed anyway. That will teach me. I'm probably getting too old for this kind of thing. One day I'll get down and won't be able to get back up. Now, what were you asking me?"

The moment was gone, though, and she didn't want to bring it back up. "Never mind. It wasn't that big of a deal. We'll talk about it another time."

"Are you sure?"

Taryn nodded. Before she got in her car, however, she stopped and called back. "Delphina? Have there ever been any stories about...this house?"

"What do you mean, dear?"

"Oh, I don't know," Taryn tried to reply lightly. "You know, like a ghost story?"

Delphina chuckled. "I've never seen a thing here. Why, dear, have you?" A slight frown lined her face, but Taryn might have imagined it because it was gone in an instant.

"It might have been a dream," Taryn shrugged. "I can have some bad ones."

Once she was in her car and on her way down the road towards the tavern, she decided Matt must be right.

With no history of hauntings, with no apparent mystery to solve, the only other thing Permelia's ghost could possibly want with her was to stop the destruction of the tavern. But how in the world could she possibly do that? If Permelia knew of a way to get that accomplished, she was going to have to do a lot more than just show up in her window.

Chapter 8

*T*aryn passed the Anderson County Historical

Society every morning and afternoon on her way to and from Griffith Tavern. It was a squat, brick building lacking any character or charm. The county jail was located next to it. The first few times she'd driven past it, she done so with a shudder. Historical societies were a little bit of a sore spot with her at the moment, considering her last experience with one, and while she tried not to hold the one incident against all of them; well, she was human.

If she was going to get anywhere, though, she would have to suck it up. The sign said "open" and Taryn wasn't on any kind of timeframe. That was the beauty of being able to work for yourself.

A pleasant-faced, plump, middle-aged woman sat behind a desk. She was staring at a computer screen, her brown hair reflecting the virtual glow. Wearing a bright pink Branson T-shirt, cartoon cat earrings dangling from her ears, and nursing something out of an Elvis mug she was a veritable display of colors and visual arrestments. She looked up when the bells from the door chimed and sent Taryn a friendly smile. Her nametag said "Miranda." "Hi there," she welcomed. "You know who or what you're looking for?"

"Sort of," Taryn mumbled. "Well, not really."

"That's okay," Miranda laughed. "We get that a lot. Tell me a few things about your ancestor and I'll try to point you in the right direction. A lot of it's online these days."

Taryn, feeling guilty she wasn't there to research some long-dead relative, pulled up a nearby folding chair and faced the woman. "I'm not actually here to look up someone for *me*," she began. "I'm here in town painting a landscape of Griffith Tavern and, well, I'm trying to do a little bit of research on it. Get some more history."

"Oh, it's a wonderful old building, isn't it?" Miranda actually clapped her hands with glee, her face lighting up. "Such a shame it's in such disrepair and going to be torn down. And such a *hist*ory!"

"Yes, that's why I'm here," Taryn agreed. "And we're hoping it won't be torn down at all."

"You know, they say Jesse James even stayed there at one time," she whispered confidentially, even though Taryn was obviously the only one there and Jesse had been dead for, well, a very long time. If Jesse James had actually visited every single place that claimed he'd stayed there, he would have never had the time to commit all the crimes he was accused of.

"You never know..." Taryn agreed, resisting the urge to debate Jesse's past. And, who knows, he might have.

"Have you read the history book about the county?" She leaned backwards and plucked a book off a shelf beside her and held it out to Taryn. She was disappointed to see the same volume she'd already read at Delphina's.

"Yes, I read through it. Unfortunately, it didn't have a lot to say about the tavern."

Miranda sighed, shaking her head in exaggerated regret. "Yes, well, that's about all that's written about it. Of course, there's a lot of *oral* history. That's how most of us got our stories. Unfortunately, some of our older residents who

110

would have remembered the tavern in its heyday are long gone now," she added sadly.

"Right." Taryn was frustrated, realizing she was hitting a brick wall. What had she hoped to accomplish anyway? She was fumbling around in the dark and she knew it. "Well, maybe you can help me out. If I ask you some questions..."

"I can see what I know!"

"Okay," Taryn rubbed her hands together in anticipation. "The treasure."

"Just a local legend I'm afraid," Miranda replied. "If there was some sort of buried treasure it would've been unearthed a long time ago. There was some work done on the tavern a long time ago. Or she would've used it herself."

Taryn assumed "she" was Permelia Burke.

"Okay. How about any crimes she might have committed?"

"Who? Permelia?" The idea seemed to shock Miranda. Her cheeks flushed bright pink and she managed to look both appalled and scandalized. "Oh *no*. She was a lovely woman. The first female business owner in the county. You know, the couple who worked for her husband stayed on for years, even after he married her. And you know it's hard to have two women in the household trying to run the show. Nothing bad was ever said."

Well, damn. Then Permelia probably didn't have anything she wanted Taryn to help her atone for. Taryn was at a loss.

With nothing but dead ends, she tried another tactic. "Has anyone tried to get the tavern on the historic landmark list? Especially since Jesse James might have stayed there and it's one of the county's original buildings?"

"Yes, I believe the paperwork is going through right now. Of course, it takes some time. In the meantime, there's nothing that says it can't be demolished. You probably know how those things work."

Taryn sighed. She knew. Miranda leaned back in her chair and gazed at her quizzically. "Let me ask you something, dear. Is there a particular reason why you think this building should be saved? Obviously, it means a lot to us, but is there something about it we should know but don't?"

Taryn smiled. "I wish I knew something you didn't. I work with historical buildings as part of my job. People, mostly organizations and companies, call me in to paint pictures of them either before they're torn down or restored. I'm a multimedia artist. As far as this one goes, if I told you, you might just think I was crazy."

"Oh, I don't know. You might want to try me."

"It called to me," she said shyly. Saying it aloud didn't make her feel any less crazy. Miranda didn't look fazed, however.

"Oh, that's easy to understand. As someone who loves old houses and barns I've stopped many a time on the side of the road and pulled out my camera when something caught my fancy. Drives my husband insane. Interesting what calls to us and what doesn't," Miranda mused.

"It *is* interesting, isn't it? The Friends of Griffith Tavern are doing everything they can. I don't know if I can do anything to help them," Taryn explained. "I don't know the area, we don't have a lot of time, and I certainly don't have any money."

"Do any of us anymore?"

Taryn laughed. "Well, I was hoping you might have some documents or really anything I could take a look at. I'm invested in this place now and I'd like to learn more." She resisted the urge to tell her Permelia's ghost was the one encouraging this side project.

"Well, we do have some of the old guest logs from the tavern here. You're welcome to look at them, but they're probably not going to be helpful. The truth is, the inn wasn't that busy and not very profitable in the later years. Oh, it had its moments in the beginning. And during the war, of course, it was a hospital. But, just like a lot of hotels nowadays, it also had its moments of difficulties. I suspect the tavern was the real moneymaker."

"I'd like to see those guest logs anyway, if it's okay."

A few minutes later Taryn found herself sitting on one of the low, floral pattern couches and flipping through pages and pages of signatures. The dates went as far back as 1835, which was impressive if you thought about it. She loved the feel of the old paper, the heaviness of the leather-bound records. Even the penmanship was sweetly antiquated. She lightly ran her finger across one name, signed with a flourish, and closed her eyes, considering the fact that she was touching something written more than one hundred years before. The signatures might not look like much, but they were trapped in time, proof someone had been alive.

Miranda was right, though; the inn had gone through dry spells. There were times when a week or more existed between the names. Most of the guests appeared to be single men, although there were a few families and couples. No single women. It would've been unlikely in those days that a single woman would've traveled alone, and so far, without an escort.

Taryn returned the books to Miranda when she was finished and stood at her desk, trying to formulate more questions. Unfortunately, nothing more was coming to her.

Tapping her long, manicured fingers on the particleboard desk, Miranda gazed ahead of her, lost in thought. Both women were at an impasse. Finally, it came to her. "I know! LeRoy Edwards at the Boain Center. It's a nursing home," she clarified. "He's almost ninety-five years old and won't remember her at all, of course, but he remembers everything else and his daddy would have told tales about her. He's the man to talk to. Would you like to meet him?"

Taryn cursed herself on the drive to the tavern. Okay, so a huge part of her was a little peacocked at the idea of suddenly gaining some kind of sixth sense on her thirtieth birthday, like Rob had hypothesized. But even she had to admit that at Windwood Farm she almost surely wouldn't have felt as drawn to the house and events that took place there if she hadn't felt somehow connected to Clara. Her own story with Andrew wasn't equivalent to Clara's suffering, but her grief was still bubbling at the surface and surely that had something to do with the house's energy drawing out her capabilities.

She should have seen the same with Griffith Tavern.

Two single women trying to run their own businesses, both lost their husbands at a young age, both trying to make it in a man's world (historical preservation and architecture was still a man's world–regardless of the strides taken). She and Permelia: two peas in a pod.

"I'm not who you think I am," she muttered aloud when the tavern came into view. "You've picked the wrong girl. I *can't* help you."

The tavern remained quiet. She attempted to paint, but she was too distracted to concentrate. None of her colors were mixing correctly and it was mostly her fault for not paying attention. Her hands were shaking and she messed up more than once. After the third attempt at shading a downstairs window, she finally gave up for the day and put her supplies away in frustration.

It was muggy and sticky and there weren't even any cars on the road to break the monotony. She'd eaten all her snacks, mostly out of boredom and stress, and picked at a hangnail until it bled. Now she had nothing left to do. In a bigger town, she might take a day off and go to the movies or hang out at a book store. The closest town with either one of those was an hour away. The doctor she was seeing back in Nashville was treating her for depression and anxiety, sure those were causing her headaches and nerve pain. She could go back and pop one of those little pills and knock herself out for a few hours but that didn't sound enticing, either. She didn't get any kind of high off that like some people did and just woke up feeling disoriented and angry she'd missed out on half the day. And they didn't even help the pain.

I even fail at being an addict, she thought bitterly as she shoved her last duffle bag into the trunk. Taryn was feeling sorry for herself but figured she deserved it. A pity party was something she thought served a purpose on occasion and Taryn was down with that.

This was supposed to be an easy job, something that would be finished within a few weeks and help her catch up with her bills.

It didn't help that since arriving she'd had Andrew on her mind a lot and her sleep hadn't been the best. True, she'd never been what you would consider a good sleeper, but now her dreams were just stupid: a lot of running around and doing silly things. She felt worn out by the time she woke up. She couldn't focus on her work. Even her painting wasn't the best she'd done and painting was usually the one thing she could count on pulling through.

"I need a best friend," she confessed aloud, her hands on her hips. "Someone to take me out and listen to me complain."

As if on cue, a loud crash rang from inside the tavern.

"I wasn't talking to *you*," she shouted, irritated. "Great, just what I need. A BFF who's rooted in the afterlife."

She was still muttering to herself (and occasionally waving her hands in the air) as she stomped across the yard towards the tavern, the weeds brushing at her legs and leaving thin scratches.

Even Taryn hadn't possessed the gall to take a step inside the dilapidated building up until that point, it *did* look like it was on its last legs, but this time she didn't hesitate. Not even stopping to pick up a snake stick in case she met a creepy crawlie inside, she hoisted herself through one of the front windows (careful not to touch the broken glass) and found herself standing in a shadowy entry. Once inside she could see the hoisting hadn't been necessary: the front door wasn't barred in any way and was almost rotted through. The boards creaked under her weight and she could hear something scurrying. It sounded too big to be a mouse.

"I'm here," she called, hands on her hips. "Now, how can I be of service?"

Chapter 9

*T*he inn, of course, was silent.

"I see, playing it coy are we?" Taryn asked, dusting off her legs from the cobwebs she'd caught on her way in. Now that she was actually inside she could get a better look around. She cursed the fact she'd brought neither Miss Dixie nor a flashlight but she hadn't exactly planned this little adventure.

The foyer floors, at least, were in better condition than she'd reckoned. They were noisy when she moved but felt solid enough and didn't appear to have any visible rot or soft spots. She'd still tread carefully. A staircase ran up the wall to her right and disappeared onto a landing. The bead board at the bottom was more detailed than she'd expected to find and the bannister appeared to be mahogany. It was in excellent condition; she could tell that even from under the layers of dust. A few hearty shakes didn't make it move. At some point someone had decided to make the unfortunate decision to carpet the stairs and mice had made good work out of the material. Hardwood peeked through where the carpet was worn away. What was left of it was covered in rodent droppings, dust, and leaves. In fact, from where she stood, she was almost certain she could see the carcass of what had once been a possum on the sixth step up.

A few cautious steps to the left took her into a parlor. It was small and empty but the curling wallpaper made her smile. When she touched it, bits crumbled into her hand. By the thickness there must have been at least three or four layers. She used to collect wallpaper samples from old houses. She'd been a child when wallpapering had still been popular; her grandmother claimed it was a pain in the ass but Taryn liked it a lot more than paint.

A fireplace was gathering more rodent excrement and dried leaves but she could still imagine weary travelers coming in from a long wagon or carriage ride and warming up by a blazing flame while they waited for someone to take their money and ready a room for them. The space was small but cozy and she was already mentally decorating with a chair, small table, and bookshelf.

A long, narrow hallway ran the length of the building but it was incredibly dark and she was only able to peek into the other rooms for fear of running into something she shouldn't (she was more afraid of spiders at this point than ghosts). There wasn't much to see. The rooms were empty and covered in dust and it was difficult to tell what they would've been.

She wasn't afraid inside, especially since by all accounts this ghost seemed to like her and want her there, but she didn't want to risk tripping over something silly like a board and end up breaking her neck. She wasn't the adventurer she'd been in her teens and early twenties.

Taryn cautiously made her way to the end of the hallway where she came to a small, narrow back staircase and the actual tavern. Of course, she'd seen the tavern from peeking in through the windows outside but it was different from this angle. Now, with the murky shadows and dimming light it felt less abandoned and more like it might be sleeping.

Because the room was empty, its openness was a testament to the number of people it could have held. It was bigger than it looked from the outside. For a moment Taryn allowed herself to imagine it alive and bursting with energy. She could hear the clinking of glasses, the stomping of feet and rustling of skirts as men and women walked back and forth across the pine floors. She saw maids in dark uniforms scurrying up the back staircase, taking some boarder his nightcap or a bowl of soup to warm his bones in the middle of a cold night after everyone else had gone to bed. She smelled the yeasty aroma of beer as it flowed across the tables and filled the bellies of both travelers and locals who had come out for the night to enjoy the company of others. There was probably a lot of music and dancing when the occasion called for it. On those nights she could see the tables pushed back, a makeshift stage set up in the corner, and hear the clapping and laughing as the patrons spun in wild circles around the room, filling the entire building with the sounds of their merriment, the walls vibrating with their vitality.

Now, the only sounds she heard were the faint scuttling of mice feet as they climbed up the walls and the chattering and hissing of what she thought might be a raccoon.

Taryn was more hesitant about climbing the stairs, especially since a large portion of the roof was missing which meant at least some of the floors were exposed to the elements, but since she'd already come this far she was game to give it a try. Still, the back ones looked a little rough for wear so instead of pressing her luck she made her way back to the front of the house.

These stairs didn't look hazardous, just dirty. She'd been on worse. She hoped if the building did get torn down someone would at least come in and save the bannister. It could be reused.

Her gut instinct about the second floor proved to be valid. She didn't trust her luck to go much further past the landing at the top of the second flight of stairs. The floor was completely rotted through in several places in the hallway and she could see sky through the roof. Birds had built their nests and forgotten them in the rafters. Still, from where she stood she could make out at least four good-sized rooms, possibly five. Permelia and her husband probably would have slept up there, unless she'd missed a room down by the tavern end, and that would have given them at least four guest rooms. Not bad for a small bump in the road.

But a big place to run on your own.

Well, she'd satisfied her curiosity of the place. It would take some work to get it back in shape, but nothing was impossible. Taryn *had* seen worse, but just barely. Permelia hadn't manifested or given her a list of people to visit who might want to donate to the cause so Taryn wasn't real sure where to go from there. Still, she always enjoyed seeing the inside of a new place so it wasn't an altogether wasted trip. To be fair, she hadn't been sure what to expect; she'd just gone in on a hunch.

Turning, she started back down the steps and was halfway to the bottom when a sound caught her ear. It could have just been the wind, or an animal, but for a second it sounded like laughter or perhaps music coming from the back of the building. Pausing mid-step, Taryn held her breath and listened again. *There*, she thought, *I'm* not *hearing things!* It was ever so slight, but it was definitely the hum of an old piano followed by the tinkling of laughter. It echoed through the empty house with a hollow resonance, a radio from far away. Picking up her pace, she hurried down the rest of the stairs in an attempt to catch the source of the sounds before they disappeared.

And landed flat on her face at the bottom.

"Damn it!" she cried in frustration, cursing her clumsiness.

Irritated with herself, as she rose up to her now skinned and aching knees and pulled her foot out from under her, she glared at the last step–the one that caught her. There was nothing on it to make her trip; in her hurry she'd merely been careless. Now, her clothes were caked with dirt and God knew what else and the sounds of the house were present-day, the laughter and piano gone. She'd missed whatever ghostly party was happening.

Standing up, she dusted herself off as best she could and grimaced at the sight of blood starting to run down her calf. She'd have several more bruises by the time evening rolled around.

"Now I just need to go back and get myself a bath," she grumbled.

As she climbed back through the window and let herself out, she couldn't be sure but thought she might have heard the faintest sigh of longing.

When Taryn arrived back at the B&B she was surprised to find she had three voicemail messages flashing on her phone. She usually had a pretty good signal at the tavern. The calls must have come through while she was creeping about.

The first one was from Matt, just checking on her. He'd followed up the call with a text and some silly joke about baking bread. She wasn't sure she got it, but she appreciated the attempt to make her laugh. The second call was from Daniel who sounded rejected and defeated. "No good news to report," he spoke forlornly into her mailbox. "Just keeping you updated."

The third call was from Miranda at the historical society. "Hi Karen!" she called cheerfully. Taryn rolled her eyes. "I just wanted to let you know I spoke to LeRoy up at the nursing home and he said he'd be glad to talk to you and tell you what he knows." Her message rambled on as she left the facility's phone number and directions and then ended up with jovial "Toodles!"

Taryn was excited to go up to the nursing home and pay LeRoy a visit. She didn't know what to expect, but any lead was worth exploring at this point. It didn't feel right, however, to leave Daniel out. After all, this was his project and his organization that was so intent on saving the tavern— he had the right to know as much about it as she did.

Daniel picked up on the first ring and didn't sound any happier than he had on her voicemail. "I really thought something might come through at the last minute; you know, like in the movies," he complained.

"It still could," Taryn hoped she sounded positive. "You never know."

They spent a few minutes talking about grants and funding until Taryn was finally able to bring the conversation back around to her original purpose. "Listen, I've been doing research on the tavern and a woman at the historical society hooked me up with an older gentleman down at the nursing home. Miranda thinks he might be helpful. I was going to try to go tomorrow and talk to him. I know it's last minute, but are you interested?"

Daniel didn't even hesitate. "Sure! Let's do it! It will need to be in the morning because I'm working tomorrow afternoon but I'd love to. We've talked to a few people here and there and looked at all the records, but nobody down there at the rehab and nursing home."

"Did you go to the historical society here?"

"Yeah, that's one of the first places I started at," he conceded. "They had a little bit, but mostly just financial records and stuff like that. A guest log."

A quick call to the nursing home let her know LeRoy was up and ready for the day every morning for breakfast, at 7:00 am sharp and that he loved having visitors. Taryn assured the nurse she wouldn't be there, up and ready for the day, at 7:00 am but that she and Daniel would be there by 10:00 am.

"That's just fine, sweetie," the nurse spoke with sugar into the phone. "And I'm sure he'll be excited to see you. He loves having young people come over to talk, especially about the old days."

Daniel hadn't questioned why Taryn had developed such an interest in the tavern, especially since she knew virtually nothing about it before arriving, but she was sure he'd eventually ask her. She was preparing an answer for him along the lines of helping her get in the right frame of mind for painting and visualizing the way it would have looked in the past.

Something told her he might have understood the ghost thing a little easier than some. But, as much as she wanted to talk about it, she was also leery of spreading the good news with just anyone. She still felt a little crazy herself.

Nevertheless, she'd been surprised at some of the reactions she'd received. Before her experience at Windwood Farm, she didn't know so many people were accepting of the ghost stories and hauntings. She should have realized it, of course. With all the shows on everything from the SyFy channel to the local cable access channels hosting ghost hunting shows and interviews with mediums, the paranormal was "hot" at the minute and it seemed, from her vantage point anyway, that these days it was more couth to share a ghost story than to admit you didn't believe in them. Almost like a reverse Salem witch trial.

With a "Real Housewives of Atlanta" marathon on, Taryn settled into the rocking chair by the window in her room and booted up her laptop. She was probably going to lose some brain cells, but she'd always thought it was best to mix up the worries of the day with something brain-numbing and mindless and there was nothing that did it better than listening to women she didn't know screaming at each other in posh settings.

Without Miss Dixie she hadn't taken any shots inside the house and now she was kicking herself. She was certain something would've popped out at her had she aimed it in a few of those empty rooms.

But she'd have to leave ghost chasing for another day. Right now, there was work to do.

Matt had emailed her a few random "Star Trek" jokes (she didn't get them, either), several people wanted her to do a "quick sample sketch" of their family house for free, and one lone email stood out with an "urgent" subject line she almost ignored but then thought better of.

She nearly dropped her computer and had to read the message four times before it sunk in.

Dear Miss Magill,

*My name is Arron Whitehouse and I am terribly
sorry to be tracking you down like this. I simply had no
other means of contacting you since the phone number and
address your aunt had on file were no longer valid. I am the
estate lawyer for Sarah Magill, your aunt, and I regret to
inform you of her recent passing. She had been sick for
some time, I have been told, but passed away peacefully in
her own home with an attending home health nurse eight
days ago. She has left provisions for you in her will, if you'll
be so kindly to contact me.*

*Again, I am so very sorry for this impersonal means
of communication. If you'd give me a call I'd be more than
happy to discuss any particulars about her passing and her
estate.*

*Thank you,
Arron Whitehouse, Esquire*

Taryn was dumbfounded. She hadn't seen her aunt in
years and therefore had no idea she was ill. She did send her
Christmas cards when she remembered but Taryn had never
been one to take the time to write her return address on
them. She assumed Sarah knew how to find her.

Setting her laptop aside, Taryn pulled her legs and
feet up into her chair and slowly rocked back and forth. Was

it cancer? A heart attack? Sarah was always something of a recluse but she'd been active, fit even. The memories Taryn had were of Sarah gardening, hiking up the mountains behind her New Hampshire home to show Taryn the view from the top, swimming in the ice cold volcanic lake—smiling as she dove off rocks and paddled her kayak at sunset. Gone? It didn't seem possible. She was the last family member Taryn had. She'd always meant to contact her, visit her, keep in touch better. Now she never would.

And what about her estate? Unless she'd been even stranger than the people of her township thought, Sarah didn't have money. She didn't really believe in it. The house was almost falling down around her the last time Taryn saw it and that was twenty years ago. She couldn't imagine what kind of shape the old farmhouse would be in now. But there would be furniture, personal papers, and other things to contend with. She'd have to call that attorney.

Why am I always surrounded by death, Taryn asked herself as she wandered down the stairs, in a daze. She didn't feel like working now. Even "Real Housewives" was losing its charm.

She meant to go outside and have a seat on the front porch, but a noise made her hesitate. Trying to walk softly on the old hardwood floors, Taryn crept to the front door and peered outside. There, the usually sunny Delphina sat in one of the white wicker chairs, her bandaged hand shaking. She was wracked with sobs she wasn't even trying to muffle and the tears ran smoothly down her lined face, one after another.

Not wanting to embarrass her, and recognizing when someone wanted a moment to themselves, Taryn turned around and climbed back up the stairs. *It must be a night of grief*, she sighed as she slipped into bed and pulled the covers up to her chin. The sadness was a second blanket.

Chapter 10

I have no idea what his mental capacity is but

Miranda said he likes to talk," Taryn warned Daniel as they climbed up the nursing home stairs. She'd had a restless night and wasn't feeling like herself. The shock of Sarah's death was still fresh and Taryn spent most of the evening trying to make some sense out of the news. She'd failed.

As far as nursing homes went, this didn't look terrible. At least the flowers and swings in the front made it look like someone was making an effort. Still, when her time came, Taryn hoped she didn't have to be put in one. She was sure the nurses and staff were qualified and caring but the idea of being cooped up, unable to come and go as she pleased, and incapable of taking care of herself scared her more than dying. At least Sarah'd been able to die in her house, amongst her belongings.

"I talked to the historical society, a lot," Daniel complained. "Nobody ever told me about this guy."

"Maybe you didn't do the secret knock," Taryn suggested with a laugh. Daniel grinned at her. She noticed he'd cleaned up some for the visit and wore pressed khakis, a Polo shirt, and had trimmed his beard. His toes still peeked out from ratty sandals, though.

"Ha! Maybe," he shrugged. "You wouldn't believe some of the walls we've hit with this project."

"I can imagine."

Low generic music was playing in the lobby and a receptionist sat behind a tall counter. She appeared to be in her early twenties and was pecking at a computer, bobbing her blond head in time to the music and sipping on a Sprite when they reached her. A bulletin board above her was covered in pictures of the residents on outings, having birthday parties, and visiting with their friends and family. Another one was decorated with laminated cutouts of fall leaves.

"Hi," Taryn started brightly. "We're here to see LeRoy–"

"He's ready!" the receptionist sang with a huge coral smile, cutting her off. "Been ready all morning. They've already taken him to the inner garden. I'll show you!"

"Peppy little thing, isn't she?" Daniel remarked under his breath as she led them down oddly quiet corridors still managing to buzz with activity at the same time.

Taryn was able to peek into a few rooms along the way and was met with a mixture of smiles, waves, and blank stares. Some residents watched television while others dozed in their chairs or on their beds. A few moaned in pain. If she were perfectly honest with herself, she was a little afraid of nursing homes and what they entailed. They were a reminder of her mortality even more than the old structures she worked with and ghosts she was starting to encounter.

The "inner garden" was a lovely area, though, and filled with stone statues, garden gnomes, little fountains pouring over fake rocks, and fragrant flowers. Several picnic tables were set up throughout the space enclosed by the home's walls. Only one man was enjoying it today, however, and he rested in a wheelchair pushed up next to a bubbling fountain. A book of Poe's short stories was on his lap.

"LeRoy, your guests are here!"

Without turning around, he raised his hand in a wave. "Well, bring them here then. It might look like I've got all day but who knows...I could die in a minute."

"He's healthy as a horse," the receptionist whispered. "Just grouchy. You'll like him, though."

LeRoy was a small man and probably appeared even slighter than he was, thanks to the wheelchair. His arms, which showed through his rolled up chambray shirt, were stained a dark brown by the sun and he still maintained a full head of wiry silver hair. While his voice might have been gruff, his bright smile betrayed him and his dentures gleamed in the sun when Taryn and Daniel sat across from him on a stone bench.

"Well, they told me I had visitors but didn't tell me one was going to be a movie star," he bellowed, casting an appraising glance at Taryn. "Ain't seen a prettier thing in years!"

Taryn blushed and Daniel laughed. "Oh, you're being nice," she scoffed.

"Too old to be nice," he muttered, running his gnarled fingers across the cover of his book. "Did that in my younger days. Now it's bad for the constitution. This here your husband?" He jerked his finger in Daniel's direction as his gaze traveled disapprovingly down to his bare toes.

"No sir, we're just working together," Daniel explained. "She let me tag along."

"Get used to it, boy," he cracked. "It don't get any better. You'll be following women around for the rest of your life."

"Thank you for taking the time to meet with us," Taryn interjected. "We appreciate it."

"Nurse says you want to talk to me about history. About the town and what-all I know."

"Well," Daniel began, "we actually want to know about a specific place. Griffith Tavern. We're working there, see, and trying to get the money to renovate it. Maybe reopen it as an events center and museum."

"Uh huh," LeRoy said, wisps of his hair fluttering with the movement. "Lot of people into that these days, the historical preservation. I seen it on all the TV programs. My roommate keeps it on the HGTV channel. A bunch of people trying to fix up houses and spending God knows how much on kitchens and bathrooms."

"Well, we think preserving this piece of history is important. And it's a wonderful building. A shame it's just falling apart," Taryn added. She liked this man. He was a little ornery, but so her grandmother had been as well. At least he was honest.

"A'course it wasn't in its prime in *my* lifetime, I'm not that old, but I heard lots of tales about it from my Pap and Grandpap. Uh huh." He pronounced "heard" as though he'd just tacked a "d" on the end of "hear." "So what-all you wanting to know about it?"

"We basically want to know what the history books don't tell us," Taryn explained. "What was it like? What were the owners like? Did people love it? Were they sad when it closed? What was its personality?"

"You're asking the right questions," he smiled. "You musta felt something from it to make you want to know. Those aren't the kind of questions they teach you to ask in school."

Taryn started to protest but he interrupted her. "Naw, it's okay. Some buildings call to you. I understand. I always thought a building was like a person myself. Had a brain and even a heart. The good ones anyway. And maybe some of the not-so-good ones."

Taryn smiled, relieved. "That's exactly what I think." A look passed between the two of them, however, that was not lost on Daniel. *He knows something about me*, Taryn thought self-consciously. *He knows there's more to it than that.*

"Well, I'll tell you what I know..." Reaching over to a small table he took a good long drink of what appeared to be lemonade and then smacked his lips. Settling back into his chair, he closed his eyes and began to speak.

"Her husband bought it and had it running, of course, but it was Permelia Burke that done gave it the life it needed. A woman can do that, you know. Women give life to things in different ways, not just by making babies. That's one of life's great mysteries. Before she come, it was wood and stone. She brought its heart."

Taryn cocked her head to one side, considering. She didn't think she'd ever heard women described in that manner before. It was...right.

"In the early days, it was the post office. Mail man would come riding in and stay a night. Get the mail delivered. That was the most important thing back then."

"Mail?" Daniel asked. "That was the most important thing? I would've thought food, supplies, even ammo."

"Well, you might take communication for granted nowadays with your interwebs and email net but there was a time when you couldn't just punch in a few numbers and talk to someone across town, much less across country. Truth be told, it was the mail service that made this country what it is today," LeRoy divulged, looking at both Taryn and Daniel with steely eyes.

"How do you reckon?" Daniel asked again, amused.

"Sharing of ideas, boy! Passing the news. Keeping connected with one another. Without a connection in this world, you don't have nothing! Just a bunch of little hamlets spread from here to Kingdom Come without any way of communicating with one another. But with the mail, you weren't so alone anymore. You were part of a bigger whole."

Daniel was silent for a minute and then nodded his agreement. "You're right. I guess I never thought of it like that. So the mail carrier, he made sure the people coming out west were connected with the folks back home? Learned things?"

"That's what I'm saying. And made sure the people back home knew what it was like out here. Talked politics, weather, babies…Even the simple things were important. But then Permelia come. She was a little bitty thing, not hardly taller than a child. He sent off for her from Boston or thereabouts in one of those publications where men of that time sometimes sought their mates. Like a personal ad as you'd call it now. A mail order bride. She came by stagecoach a couple hours from here and he went to pick her up. They got married there and he brought him back a wife nobody here'd seen the likes of.

"Now, you must remember that back in those times this was a rough place. Only a few houses, one store, and the post office. Not too many women. This was a stopover point for people heading up east and further west. This used to be the Wild West, you know, before too many folks got brave and went further. They'd started putting in the railroad, of course, but it stalled. And then the war come. Bet you didn't know the inn was a hospital for a time, did you?"

Both Taryn and Daniel shook their heads and looked at each other.

LeRoy, enjoying his importance now, nodded. "Oh yes. And that would even be after the mister passed on. She would've run it during then, too. Of course, I'm getting off track. Not too many people staying here for long to make it their home. Some families come through but it was mostly men, maybe staying a night or two."

Taryn imagined the transient nature of the tavern and inn must have been both exciting and sad. It would've been difficult for Permelia to have made friends. She wondered how she'd adjusted to this lifestyle, especially after having lived in Boston all her life.

"With Permelia here in her fancy dresses and fixed hair and pretty shoes the menfolk finally had something to look at. She was more than just a pretty face, though. She could cook up a storm and that's partly why people started staying longer than a night. She had a kitchen manager, I guess you'd call 'em that nowadays, but it was Permelia's cooking that everyone wanted.

"I always heard they never turned anyone away. Fix 'em up a pallet in the parlor or out in the barn if they needed to. Didn't want anyone staying out in the cold. Nobody had nothing bad to say about either one of them. They was good folks. Decent. That's what I always heard."

"It's funny how a person's reputation continues to live on, even after they've been dead for over one hundred years," Taryn mused aloud.

"Yep. Both good and bad," LeRoy agreed. "So you have to watch how you behave, what you say, if you want that reputation to be a good one after you're gone."

"The parties came later," he continued, "'balls' Permelia called 'em, even though they wasn't much more than some fiddlers, banjo pickers, and whiskey flowing. She'd put on one of them pretty dresses and float around, making sure everyone was happy and didn't need anything.

"Later, more inns were built, we got a proper post office, and some stores popped up in town. More people building their houses and staying. Farmers mostly. A paper mill came later, but that was much later—in my lifetime. After the war the railroads took off. Put an end to the stagecoach stop part of it."

"And when her husband died?" Taryn prodded.

"Just an accident. Probably broke her heart. From all accounts they was truly in love with each other. Might have been a cold marriage from the start, but my Grandpap said they was always stealing kisses with each other, he was hugging her up in front of others, and she smiled at him when she thought he weren't looking. At the balls they'd dance a waltz or a polka and make everyone smile.

"The inn traffic had slowed down a little before he died and the tavern wasn't getting as much business with other ones sprouting up. Then, with a less person to help out, it looked like it might close. People wondered what would happen to Permelia. Some thought she'd go back east to her family. She didn't, though. Just rolled up her sleeves and kept it going. Kept it up until she died," he shrugged. "She had some tragedy in her life, I can tell you that."

"Losing her husband at a young age," Taryn agreed.

"Yep, that," he said. "Hard having a baby in those times, too."

Taryn and Daniel looked up sharply. "Baby?" they echoed.

"Oh yes, a baby. Not real sure what happened to it. Pretty little thing, though. My Grandpap said my Granny knitted it booties."

"So there's a descendent roaming around somewhere?"

LeRoy's eyes twinkled. "T'would appear that way, wouldn't it? But I just don't know."

LeRoy stopped talking then and closed his eyes. His head was starting to droop a little and his hands were shaking. Taryn, sensing the end of the story, exhaled. She hadn't realized she'd been holding her breath. "When she died, did she leave a lot of money?"

"Not that I know of," he replied softly. "She wasn't in debt or anything but there wasn't nothing screaming riches either. Some other folks took over, tried to keep it up, but it was never the same. When I was a young'in I remember it being an inn for awhile and a tavern but it was just another place to go. Nothing special about it. Nothing like it would've been a century before."

"I wonder how she was able to keep it going like she did, with business so slow," Daniel mused.

"Lots of people wondered the same thing," LeRoy clucked his tongue. "Running a business back then wasn't a whole lot different than it is now. Always been hard work."

"I hear that," Taryn agreed.

"And what do you do, missy?" he asked.

Taryn did her best to give him an abbreviated version of her career and what some of her duties consisted of.

"And you got no man to help out with any of it?" he asked carefully when she was finished.

"No sir. My husband passed away several years ago. We were a team while he was alive, though."

LeRoy shook his head. "No wonder the house calls to you."

Back in the parking lot Daniel gave Taryn a quick, slightly awkward, hug. "I'm sorry about your husband," he said shyly, his cheeks a little flushed. "I didn't know."

"It's okay," she shrugged. "It's not something I normally go around announcing. I think the visit went well, though. I liked LeRoy." She didn't exactly want the afternoon to turn into a "poor Taryn" love fest. That would've been uncomfortable for both of them.

"Yeah, yeah, it was great! Just hearing someone talk about the place, and not having to read about it in stuffy archives, has made me excited all over again. Wouldn't it be great to bring back some of its former glory?!"

Taryn allowed Daniel to carry on and talk for the next few minutes while she leaned up against her car and thought about LeRoy's stories. She'd already considered the fact Permelia might have latched onto her because they were similar in some regards, but it still didn't explain what she wanted out of Taryn. Perhaps it was nothing more than to acknowledge her, to get her story out. But Taryn was no writer. Her college professors could attest to that.

Daniel was mid-sentence, going on about how wonderful the tavern would look with new floors, when she interrupted him. "I've seen a ghost," she proclaimed in a hurry.

"What?" he asked, confusion spreading across his face. "Just *now*?"

"No, not just now. I'm sorry. I didn't mean to interrupt you. I just *have* to talk about this with someone other than my friend and, well, you've been elected. I've been seeing things. At the tavern, in my room at the B&B..." She let her voice trail off, not sure she wanted to talk about Miss Dixie and what her "talents" were.

"Wow. That's awesome. Of course I believe you. I've felt a few things at the tavern myself, but never saw anything."

"Really? What did you feel?"

"Hard to explain I guess. Like someone was watching me mostly. And once I thought I heard someone screaming. It dug right down into the pit of my stomach. The sound, I mean. Just horrible. But I talked myself out of it, told myself it must have been from somewhere else and the sound just carried. What's going on with you?"

"The stuff I'm seeing in my room? I think it's connected to the tavern. I think Permelia is trying to tell me something. Now do you think I'm crazy?"

Daniel's eyes widened. "Hell no! Me and my friends? We're totally into all of that. And LeRoy said she might feel a connection with you. Do you think that's it?"

"Yes, I do," Taryn consented. "I think she's trying to tell me something or wants me to do something. But I have no idea *what* that may be."

"Then it sounds like we have a mystery on our hands!" Daniel announced with glee.

"Well, Shaggy, go tell Fred and Daphne and we'll sort it out!" Taryn smiled wanly. "I guess we're the 'meddling kids.'"

"Can you tell me what you've seen?"

So for the next half hour Taryn and Daniel sat on the grass in front of the nursing home and talked about what was going on. She skirted around her experiences with Miss Dixie but left out little else. Daniel interrupted her a few times, wanting more detail, but for the most part he listened intently, his eyes widening at the appropriate places. When she was finished, he fell back on the ground and gazed up at the clouds.

"Geeze," he breathed. "That would've scared the shit out of me. All of it. But it has to mean something. Still, I've not come across any ghost stories with the place. You're the first, other than what I've felt. That can't be a coincidence."

"No, I don't think it is," she agreed.

"Have you always seen ghosts?"

"Well, sort of. It's complicated."

"I have time. Care to explain?"

She hesitated and then went for it. "When I was a kid I saw a little dead girl. Only, I didn't know she was dead at first. That came later. She showed me where she had died and then just kind of disappeared. It made my parents nervous and I promised I wouldn't talk about it."

"And nothing else?" he pressed. "I mean, not that *that* incident isn't enough. Just wondering if anything else pops out at you. Seems kind of off for that to happen and then quit until now."

"My friend who owns a kind of new age shop down in Kentucky said the same thing. He thinks whatever I have may have gotten stronger around my last birthday. I repressed it, I think," she explained. "If things did happen then I ignored them. Maybe explained them away until they just stopped happening altogether. But, sometimes I wonder…"

"What?"

Taryn pursed her lips and struggled to find the words. "I played games as a young child. And in hindsight I wonder if maybe they weren't *really* games. Like, when I was two, I used to pretend there was a ghost in the corner of the room. Always the same corner, always the same room. I'd see it when I visited my grandmother. She told me I'd pretend to hide and ask her to go 'get' the ghost. So, to humor me I guess, she'd run over to it and shout, 'Go away ghost, go away!' Then, after a few tries I'd do the same. But she said sometimes I looked genuinely scared and there were moments when she wasn't so sure I wasn't actually seeing something."

"Yeah, that's possible," he agreed. "Maybe you were and your young mind didn't know how to process it so you made a game out of it."

"And, for years, I had an imaginary friend. A Chinese girl named Julie." Seeing the look on his face she laughed. "Yeah, I know. It was probably the only name I could think of. It lasted for almost three years, up until I was about five. I can vaguely remember talking to her, playing with her, pretending she was there. Only..." Taryn shivered a little, remembering. "Only thinking back I can actually *see* her face. Maybe it's just something from a movie but sometimes I'm not entirely convinced I made her up."

"What happened to her?"

"One day she told me she couldn't stay any longer and she had to leave me, but that she would always love me," Taryn replied, blushing.

"So she dumped you," Daniel mused. "Yeah, that's odd. Maybe there is something to that."

"I don't know," Taryn shrugged. "Those are the only things I can think of. Definitely nothing like what's happening now."

"Sounds like enough, though," he said. "And hey, what about Permelia's baby? That came out of left field."

"Yeah, seriously," she agreed. "Maybe the baby died? It happened a lot in those days. If it had survived then you know we would've heard something..."

They were both silent now, lost in thought.

"Listen, I feel bad about you being up here by yourself. Some of us are going out tomorrow night. Why don't you come? It will be fun!"

Taryn smiled. She didn't know if it was a pity-ask or not but she appreciated the thought. "I don't get out much. Where are you going?"

"There's a bar in the next county over. Moe's. They play good music on Friday nights. We just go and have a few beers. Listen to the music and talk. You don't have to drink if you don't want to," he proclaimed in a rush.

"I'm not opposed to alcohol," she laughed. "I might not be the young whippersnapper I use to be but I can still drink. I'll try to make it if I can. I still have some work to do at the tavern. And I appreciate you asking. I do."

Chapter 11

*S*leep was a catastrophe. She shouldn't even have

tried. With nothing on television other than over-priced aprons on the home shopping network Taryn resorted to working on the painting for most of the night. As a result, by the time morning rolled around, her excitement at heading to the tavern and painting in general was low. She felt cranky, out-of-sorts, and depressed and just wanted to crawl back into bed and go to sleep. But, the sun was out and the day promised to be a pretty one. Seemed a shame to waste it sleeping.

Delphina had set out a nice breakfast spread and Taryn did her best to eat as much as possible. She also tried to respond to her chirping questions about LeRoy and the nursing home, even though she was too tired to feel sociable.

"In some ways I'm glad my dear husband didn't stick around here to get sick and end up in one of those homes," Delphina sighed. "Of course, who knows what kind of shape he's in now," she added quickly.

"I guess we all hope we don't have to go to one, although this one seemed nice," Taryn agreed as she bit into an apple cinnamon muffin.

"They all look the same to me. He was always afraid of being dependent on someone else," Delphina continued. "Didn't even care that much for me waiting on him."

"Delphina, do you have any idea where he might have gone?" It seemed so strange he would have just upped and left after all those years of marriage without a word.

"A few ideas I suppose. He always wanted to go out west and see the Tetons, visit Montana. When I think of him, that's where I imagine he is. Somewhere exciting."

"I feel bad for you. I mean, I don't pity you," Taryn added quickly, feeling thoughtless. "I just feel bad that you're all alone. And that he would do that and leave you behind."

"We all have our secrets, dear. We all have our skeletons in the closet. He had his. How well can we really know anyone?" Delphina whispered, her frail old hand stopping to glide over a small teacup on a sideboard. "I don't

153

know where his spirit is now but I hope it's peaceful somewhere."

With that, she walked out of the room and Taryn didn't see her again for the rest of the day.

The call from Miranda came as she was driving out to the tavern. She'd been expecting some sort of follow-up after her visit to the nursing home.

"I hear your visit went well, sweetie," she cooed into the phone.

Taryn knew it was wrong to talk on the phone and drive–that's why she put her phone on speaker. And she knew it was still bad, and probably illegal, but she hoped (probably like everyone else did) she wouldn't get caught.

"I think so," she called downwards into her lap as she sped along the asphalt. "I had a nice time. Thank you for doing that for me."

"Oh, it's no problem. He enjoys visitors. Listen, I did something else. I hope you don't mind," she chirped. "We did have a little bit of a family tree on Permelia. It isn't much, just some names, but I went ahead and emailed them to you."

"Wow, thanks!"

"Now these aren't going to be direct descendants you understand," Miranda warned, "since they didn't have any children, but these are the names of a brother and a sister. If you know anyone who has genealogy skills you might get lucky."

Taryn sat back in her seat, a little stunned. "Well, thank you. Yeah, I appreciate it. Really." She started to tell her what LeRoy had said about the baby but for some reason bit her tongue. She wanted to ruminate on that some more.

"Of course, we'd do it ourselves, but we're very busy here you understand and since they don't have anything to do with our own town..."

"No, that's fine. It's okay. I'll find someone," Taryn assured her.

When she clicked off and turned on the radio she found Iris Dement singing "Sing the Delta" on NPR. The slow, bluesy melody and her strong vocals filling the car with passion. With a new enthusiasm, Taryn turned the knob up as loud as she could stand and sang along. The day wasn't shaping up to be so bad after all.

It had rained earlier and now the sunlight was making everything look bright and crisp around the tavern. This was usually the kind of day Taryn loved to paint in. Painting wasn't what she had in mind, though. She'd left all her paints at the B&B and, instead, brought nothing but Miss Dixie and a spare memory card. (And hiking boots this time because you could never be too cautious.)

After lovingly taking her out of the camera bag ("Hello there, old girl") and slamming the car door shut she turned and faced the poor old building. If anything, it looked more wretched in the bright sunlight which did nothing to hide its flaws and mistreatment. Now that she knew more about its history, her feelings for it were personal. They had a connection now.

With solid resolution, Taryn marched across the damp grass, grasshoppers and tree frogs skipping out of her way. She talked to herself as she walked.

"Okay, obviously you want something from me and I'm going to try to help you, like you asked. And by 'you' I don't know if I'm talking to a ghost-you or a memory-you or a house-you so you're going to have to work with me a little bit on this one." The tavern remained still.

When she reached the front porch she stood in the tall grass, hands on her hips, and surveyed the tavern. "I wish I knew where to start, but I don't. Unless you have some sort of buried treasure around here to reveal to me I don't know what I can do for you. But I'll try."

So, Taryn did what she did best. She started with the front porch and, once again, worked her way around the building, snapping pictures as she went. Although she'd already done this once, and twice if you wanted to count the time her camera wasn't with her, this time she tried to capture the energy and anything else she might be able to pick up as she worked.

She didn't just take pictures of the whole structure; she zoomed in on the details. Like a person, a building was the sum of its parts. Every little element was important. Taryn never forgot this and neither did Miss Dixie. It was part of what made her a good photographer and a lot of what made her an excellent painter.

As she snapped photos of the windows, the ivy, the storm cellar door (she wasn't going down there—that was just too much), and the back awning, she tried to imagine Permelia and James getting up at dawn and preparing meals, sweeping off the steps, greeting visitors. She imagined the sounds of hoof beats as they trotted down the dirt drive, ready to deliver mail to those who had been waiting for weeks, or maybe even months for word from back home.

She stood at the back and observed the towering second floor and imagined a faint light in Permelia's window, a lantern or something, and its paleness flickering in the dark. What would James have felt, outside in the night, looking up at this window and knowing that his wife awaited him? What were the sounds here? What would guests have heard? Horses bellowing in the distance, chickens clucking (there was an ancient chicken coop in the back, after all), pots and pans rattling through the open windows? Guests laughing, singing, calling to one another from across the lawn?

What would people have *seen*? The building had changed, but the view hadn't, not really. Someone who had stood in this exact location one hundred years ago would've felt the same ground under their feet, looked up at the same sky and moon, seen the same things she was seeing now– minus the modern additions, of course. She tried to capture that, too. Therein laid the bulk of Taryn's talent: the ability to see and feel what decades and even centuries separated her from.

Once she'd circled the perimeter she let herself back inside. Although no longer afraid the place was going to fall in on her, she did watch her step and tread carefully. Daniel and Matt would not be pleased if she wound up in the hospital. Again.

Soft shadows played on the hardwood floors and while most of the rooms were dark, either from having their windows boarded up or being overgrown with vines, she'd come prepared for that with her mini flashlight. Of course, things weren't going to look *exactly* the same as when Permelia'd been running the place. It had gone through several hands since then. The walls were papered over who knew how many times, there was some hideous green shag carpet in one room that smelled horrendous and looked worse, and (now that she got a closer look) it appeared electricity was even installed somewhere along the way.

But that wasn't the point.

With any luck, Miss Dixie would pick up on the old energy, the one *under* the layers. That was Miss Dixie's talent. Things may change, but nothing ever really died. She'd already learned that. You can cut your hair, get a tan, and change your outer appearance but what forms inside your mind never truly goes away–it just found a cupboard or box to hide in. (Still, a good dye job never hurt when it came to your mental health.)

She wanted to check her LCD screen after each shot but restrained herself. She'd force herself to wait until she returned to her room. If she looked now, it might either freak her out or cause some kind of chasm which would stop whatever was going on—if anything *was* happening at all. There was always a chance Miss Dixie wasn't picking up on anything.

Taryn knew she was, though. From the moment her foot hit the second floor landing the hair on the back of her neck had stood up at point, like little icy fingers were tugging at it. The feeling began at the nape of her neck and carried upwards in a wave until her entire head was tingling, the curls in her hair almost bouncing. There was a viscosity in the air up there not caused by being closed in or shut off from the rest of the world. You could taste it; it was sour, musty, and had just a tinge of bitterness. And yet...it wasn't entirely unpleasant.

She'd originally thought the floors too rotten to wander past the landing but now she took her chances. By stepping lightly and walking around the softest parts she was able to explore the upstairs.

As Taryn wandered through each of the small rooms, presumably former guest rooms, and aimed Miss Dixie into the darkness, the thickness grew warmer and thicker until it enveloped her in a cocoon. It was comforting in a sense, this swallowing, and she almost felt as though she were floating now, carried along not by her feet but by the stale, hollow air she traveled through.

Was she dreaming? Taryn didn't think so. She knew she was awake and yet had the oddest sensation of not being in control of her movements. The dull headache that usually played at the edge of her temple subsided. Her joints, often stiff and throbbing these days (probably from hunching over at her computer and canvas) were fluid. The sense of euphoria that became her shroud was similar to the one she'd briefly experienced while on the morphine the hospital gave her after being whacked in the head over the summer.

She let the feelings carry her and did little more than aim her camera and shoot. She wasn't afraid; she didn't feel much of anything at all. There was no sense of terror even though she could barely see where she was walking (and the squishiness under her feet told her she had stepped on more than one dead animal) and she was alone.

Finally, when she reached the back of the house, she stopped in what had more than likely been Permelia and James' room. It was slightly larger than the others, though smaller than it once was since part of it had been sectioned off to make a modern bathroom with a dated pink bathtub and sink. The middle of the floor had rotted through, revealing a large gaping hole that looked down into the tavern.

It would've been noisy in this room. Nobody could've slept as long as customers were down below. Then again, it

161

might have been nice to lie there in bed and listen to the live music or the laughter. Nice, or maybe lonesome. Strange to think whoever was in this room could've heard whatever was going on below but the people down below wouldn't have heard any noises above them. Living apart from the world in general like that was surreal. Taryn felt like she did that every day.

Taryn stood still and closed her eyes, letting the atmosphere of the room cloak her.

For a brief moment she had an image of a woman with dark hair lying on a four poster bed, the thick covers brought up to her chin as she gazed at flickering candlelight making crazy patterns on her wall. She was new here, only just arrived the day before. She was married but didn't know her husband. They'd only just met. Homesick, she missed her family and house and friends. She missed the movement and sounds of the city, the familiarity of her surroundings. Her husband seemed kind, but they hadn't known what to say to one another on the ride. He'd left her alone this evening while he tended the tavern. She'd stayed here, in their bedroom, and written a letter to her family at the small desk. She'd told them everything was fine, that it was a lovely place, and that she was happy. Then she'd slid down to the floor and cried; cried loudly since with the ruckus below nobody could hear her and it didn't matter. Now she was in bed, wearing a gown from her trousseau, and listening to the sounds. So many people down there, yet she was more alone than she'd ever been in her life.

Taryn jumped, startled. She wasn't sure if it was her imagination making her see and feel what she was sensing or something else, but it felt *real*. She had a strong sense of affection for Permelia in that instant, despite the fact she knew Permelia had eventually gone on to become a lively hostess who was adored by her husband (by accounts anyway) and an astute businesswoman who hadn't even returned to Boston once he passed away.

She took her last two pictures in the room and then left. Before starting back down the stairs, however, she paused at the first room at the top. Something was pulling at her, beckoning her to return to it.

It was the smallest of the rooms. She'd only spent a minute in it earlier, maybe less. It was dark and stuffy. A dead bird was in the middle, its feathers peppering the floor, its glassy eyes staring at her. That wasn't what caught her interest, though. Even with her camera lowered she could see the shapes emerging on the wall before her. First dim, almost transparent, and then gradually growing stronger and stronger until, like watermarks, they jumped out and stained the floral wallpaper. Taryn's hand shot to her mouth as she gasped first and then moaned. The dark substance painting the handprints before her was blood.

I was getting worried." Matt was on the verge of whining. She could hear it in his tone, but he was also truly worried. She could hear that as well.

"Oh, I'm fine," she scoffed. Balancing her phone against her neck she used her key to unlock her door and hold her six pack of Cokes without dropping her camera bag. She was just good like that. "I've just had a lot of things going on."

With nothing that could be called "grace" Taryn staggered into her room and managed to toss the carton on the bed before it landed in the floor, spewing soda everywhere. The grocery bag containing chips, chocolate chip cookies, Pop Tarts, and bananas (you know, to balance everything out) slipped neatly from her other arm and landed on the floor with a "splat." "Damn it!" she muttered.

"What? Is everything okay?"

"It's fine," she sighed as she dropped down onto the bed and rested her feet against the soda carton. "I'm just throwing things around my room."

"Oh, okay. So what's going on? Why have you been so busy?"

"Well, for starters I met with a guy who told me all about the tavern and what it used to be like. That was great. And I've been doing a lot of painting, of course. Talking to my landlady. My client asked me to meet him and his friends at a bar tonight. I might go. So a lot of things."

"Your client? You mean the guy?" He didn't do a good job of hiding the blatant curiosity, although she could tell he tried.

"Yes, but don't worry. I'm not interested in him in that way. He's too young for me," she soothed him. "You're still my number one guy."

"And we're still getting married in ten years if we're both still single, right?" Matt prodded.

"Right. When we're 'old and decrepit' as I remember us saying. Of course, we were ten at the time so forty felt a long ways off back then."

"We could always do it now," Matt ventured with a laugh. "Why wait?"

A warning bell dinged inside Taryn's head but she tried to push it away. "Because I don't have the money for a dress yet. You have to give me some time."

"Anything new on the house front?" He wasn't always the most perceptive of souls, but he usually knew when to change the subject.

"Actually, yes there is." Turning on her laptop, she waited for it to boot up while she talked. "I have some names I'd like you to trace. I know you have a lot going on, but you're very good at this sort of thing and it would help me out."

"Sure, I can try. Who are they?"

"Long lost relatives of the woman who used to own the tavern. I have no idea if they had any kids or not but I can give you names and towns and a general date range. You'll have to go from there on your own," she apologized.

"No problem. I've started with less." Although Matt's field was engineering, he was also a whiz on the computer and could research just about anything. She often went to him when she either didn't have time to do it on her own or hit a roadblock. He missed his calling as a private investigator.

"I'm anxious to get in touch with them, see if they have any more information besides what I've gathered here. It might be a dead end, but you never know."

"Wow, you're really getting into this project aren't you?" Matt sounded surprised. She'd barely said a word about her previous two jobs. She'd been in and out in a flash

166

with the projects making no perceptible impact on her. They were, in her own words, "just jobs."

"Yeah, it's interesting. I mean, not just the tavern itself although the history is pretty fascinating when you think about that time period, but with Permelia. It's obvious she wants me to help her save it but I haven't been able to piece anything together yet. And besides, I feel so sorry for her. She came here without knowing anyone, was all alone, started building a life, and then lost her husband and was then *really* all alone. It must have been a struggle for her. I can't stop thinking about her–how she felt, what she thought, if she was scared or lonely..." She stopped because she was rambling and it embarrassed her.

"Taryn," Matt began gently, "you know that's over, right? Permelia is dead and has been for a long time. You're not really helping her. She's not here anymore."

"Well, I know that," Taryn almost snapped but thought better of it. "But *something* of her is here. Leftover energy or a hologram of sorts. She's not gone completely. And this is my job. This is what I do. I see the past."

"You *paint* the past," he corrected. "That's different. You don't have to become so involved."

"But I–"

"Are you sleeping well?" he interrupted. "Are you eating okay? Don't get so involved with this that it takes over.

This isn't your time period, it's not your life. You don't have to fix this."

"I can't just do nothing. What if this *is* my life? What if this is, like, my calling? And I think she needs me."

"Taryn, Permelia lived a long time ago. She apparently had a happy life and it didn't end badly. She died from regular old-age health problems. People liked her. She ran a business. She didn't have a life full of tragedy."

"Her husband died and left her a widow, all alone in the world," Taryn spoke softly, staring at the hooked rug on the hardwood floor. "Wasn't that enough tragedy?"

Matt swore under his breath. "I'm sorry. I wasn't thinking. Of course it was a tragedy. People did die young in those days, though. It happened."

"He didn't die from a health problem; it was an accident. And people dying young doesn't make it any less sad or important to her, Matt." This time Taryn did snap. "It doesn't matter how often it happens. When it's *you* it's different."

"I know. And I'm sorry. I shouldn't have said that. Is this about Andrew? Do you feel close to her because of Andrew?" There was a softness in his voice only Matt could carry and it struck a nerve in her. She could feel the tears forming in her eyes and nose before she could stop them.

"No," she whispered.

"Do you want to talk about it?"

Andrew waking up in the morning, tickling her on the neck. Andrew making the two of them a spaghetti picnic under the oak tree with the Spanish moss in southern Georgia. Andrew studying his blueprints, a pencil tucked behind his ear and his forehead creased in concentration. She and Andrew running to the car in the pouring rain, getting soaked because they'd forgotten their umbrellas, and then laughing when they reached it and realizing they'd left their windows down.

She didn't feel like she was crying, but the tears wouldn't stop falling. "No. It's fine. I just feel so bad for her. She was by herself. She didn't know what to do or where to go. She had a business to run, a house to keep up..."

"And she did it well," Matt assured her. "She did it alone, but she managed it. And did a very good job. You've done wonderfully."

Embarrassed at her display of emotions, Taryn wiped her eyes and brought up her email. "I have the names if you have something to write them down with.

"Sure. Go ahead and give them to me and I'll see what I can do..."

Chapter 12

*T*he pictures uploaded steadily, one image

painstakingly unfolding at a time. The first few dozen were of the exterior. She wasn't as concerned with these, since in her limited experience they hadn't proved as remarkable as the interior shots. While they were uploading she wandered around her room, tidying up and organizing her things. She did turn into a slob when she traveled, despite the fact she was, by nature, fastidiously clean and orderly at home. Of course, a lot of her stuff was in storage and she was rarely home anymore so there wasn't a whole lot to mess up or time to mess it up in.

Her clothes were her biggest problem, and her biggest weakness. She just had so darn many of them. She loved her skirts, jackets, cotton dresses, western-style shirts, and jeans. And cowboy boots. You could never have too many of those. After Andrew died she'd first gone through a period in which she wanted to either wear his clothes or only wear clothes she remembered him liking or commenting on. It made her feel more connected to him. She hadn't cut her hair for the longest time for the same reason–she couldn't stand letting go of growth that had known him. Later, she did a 180 and couldn't stand to wear anything she associated with him. That, of course, meant she'd needed to buy a whole new wardrobe.

That part wasn't so bad.

A beep from the bed alerted her the uploads were finished. The room was in reasonably good shape so she scooted back over to the bed and plopped down on the comfortable duvet and stretched out, ready to be immersed in her own photography for the foreseeable future.

As she suspected, the first dozen or so shots were unremarkable in nature. There were a few good ones, she liked to give herself a little bit of credit for that, but there wasn't anything out of the ordinary in any of them.

And then she got to the interior...

Holy hell.

She should have been prepared for what she saw, but she wasn't. She thought the simple act of wanting something to happen would take the shock value out of it.

It wasn't.

Except for a few balls of light, she knew from her research some people might call them orbs but they could just as well be balls of dust, most of the rooms were unremarkable.

And then there were the others.

In the first picture she took in Permelia's bedroom, the room was empty. A thin layer of dust covered the hardwood floors and there was a pile of what appeared to be rodent bones under the window. Old plastic blinds dangled above it, looking sad and dirty. Nothing new there. The room looked exactly as she'd seen it in person.

The next picture, however, showed something completely different. The image was very faint and almost looked like a double exposure if she'd been using print film, but there was no denying the fact that a large four-poster bed took up the middle of the floor. A burgundy spread was draped over it, the edges slightly dusting the floor. The spread was turned back, revealing light-colored sheets and two pillows. Propped against one of them was the dim outline of a woman. Her hair was long and dark and fell gently to her shoulders in a fluffy crown. She wore something white, that much was clear, and held her hands at either side of her, as though she'd just been disturbed and had quickly risen from a sleeping position. The most curious thing about her, other than her very appearance, was that she appeared to be staring straight at Taryn and Miss Dixie.

"I didn't imagine her," Taryn whispered to the room. "She was there." Moreover, and this chilled her to the point she pulled her cardigan in a little tighter, Permelia (for she was certain that's who it was) sensed *her*. Again. How was it possible when she'd been dead for more than one hundred years?

Delphina was sitting in a Cracker Barrel rocking chair on the front porch, a Danielle Steele book in her thin hands, when Taryn stepped outside. At the last minute she'd decided to take Daniel up on his offer. She might be a fifth wheel amongst him and his friends but it was a nice night, he had offered, and she figured she owed it to herself to try to have a little fun. She hadn't seen or talked to Delphina recently, however, so she took the time to stop and say hello.

"Is it a good book?" she inquired, leaning up against the porch railing. "My grandmother used to read her."

"Oh, it's enjoyable," Delphina laughed. "To tell you the truth, I read a lot of classics, a lot of important books and sometimes my brain just needs a rest. This here is my guilty pleasure. At least I know what I'm getting."

"I hear that," Taryn agreed. "It's why I carry naughty romance novels around with me. Just to take my mind off things."

"I'm so sorry about your aunt," Delphina professed, clutching her chest, as though even thinking about death made her heart race. "I know we didn't have much time to talk the other day. Were you very close to her?"

Taryn felt a wave of sadness well up in her and her eyes blurred a little. "We used to be, when I was a kid. I hadn't seen her in years. That makes me feel worse."

"Well, dear, life does get in the way sometimes. We think we have time and then we don't. It's nobody's fault. I'm sure she didn't fault *you* for it."

But Taryn wasn't sure what her Aunt Sarah had thought. They'd barely spoken in years and she was starting to discover, in dismay, she barely knew the woman.

"It kind of was my fault, though," she decreed. "I always loved Sarah, idolized her. But my parents? They were...distant is the best word I can come up with. I started

174

living with my grandmother when I was pretty young. And then my grandmother died. I think I was always afraid that maybe the Sarah I had in my mind, the one I loved and looked up to, wouldn't be the same to me as an adult as she was to me as a kid. And that—"

"Scared you?" Delphina finished for her. "I can understand. You didn't want your illusions to be shattered."

"Yes," Taryn agreed with relief. "That image of her and how good she was to me, what a free spirit she was, how she accepted me...I've held onto those things over the years through some of my darkest times. And it was easy to hold onto as long as it was just in my mind. What if reality was different? I didn't want to lose that."

"Did you ever think she may have thought of you the same way?" Taryn must have looked startled because Delphina laughed a little before she continued. "Honey, we all create our own ghosts, our own illusions. Maybe she didn't want to lose the one she had of a little girl who idolized her."

Taryn nodded. Maybe that was true. Sometimes reality just wasn't worth the risk.

The bar was a twenty-five minute drive from the B&B and therefore gave Taryn plenty of time to think. That wasn't always a good thing.

To say she was nervous about hooking up with college kids and spending the evening at a bar was an understatement. She almost talked herself out of it and turned around twice. A Miranda Lambert CD she cranked up was supposed to give her something like girl power or courage but it was just making her feel silly and old. She may have only been thirty but she felt twice that. Maybe she needed to dye her hair again or something.

She could admit she didn't make friends easily; never had. This was something her mother was faintly embarrassed of; that is, when she took the time to notice her.

On her sixteenth birthday, even after she'd been living with her grandmother for awhile, her mother'd had this "fabulous" idea of throwing her a "Sweet 16 Birthday Tea" at Belle Meade, the prominent country club there in Nashville her parents belonged to. It was old and southern and she'd never been real comfortable there, but it was pretty and she did appreciate the historical nature of it and the architecture. The only problem was, she didn't have any friends to invite. Well, nobody but Matt. And her mother wanted it to be an "all girls" thing.

She put off handing out the invitations until the last minute, so mortified that she didn't have anyone to give one to. She never got invited to anyone else's parties and only had a friendly "hey, how are you?" association with most of the kids in her school. She just couldn't admit to anyone, especially herself, that nobody would want to come to her party.

She'd actually cried about that a little, and tried to seek comfort from Matt. "So?" he'd shrugged. "I don't really have friends, either, except for you. It's not like we're ever going to see these people again once we graduate." He hadn't exactly been soothing at the time.

Finally, in emotional exhaustion, she'd given the ten invitations to some girls in the Drama Club and her chorus class. She prefaced each invite with pretty much the same speech: "Hey, I know this is kind of last minute, but I'm having this birthday party at Belle Meade. I'm not inviting a lot of people, and it's just girls, but I thought maybe you'd like to come. You know, if you're not too busy. But I can totally understand if you are."

All in all, it wasn't a very exciting or convincing speech and she knew in her heart she'd have to return to her mother and tell her to cancel it. But, to her surprise, every one of those girls RSVP'd.

Maybe they liked her more than she realized. Maybe she had more friends than she knew!

Nah, it was the lure of attending a function at Belle Meade that did it in the end. Nobody wanted to pass that up. They might have only been teenagers, but their parents were impressed enough to highly encourage them not to turn it down.

All in all, the tea was a success. The food was delicious, the private dining room beautiful, and the conversation cheerful. They'd laughed and joked about teachers, about different guys they all knew, and about what the future held in store for all of them. They'd all brought presents Taryn cooed and clucked over and in the group picture the girls gathered closely around her, smiling for the camera with their beautiful, straight teeth and glossy hair. To a stranger, they all would've appeared to be best of friends.

Taryn returned home feeling happy, content, even a little high from her afternoon. Her grandmother was happy for her, her mother smug.

She'd gone to school that Monday feeling confident in her newfound friendships. And the girls were all cordial. Nobody was rude or mean to her. But none of them went out of their way to include her in anything; nobody asked her to sit with them at lunch, invited her over to their house, passed notes to her, or walked with her down the hallways. It was as though they hadn't even shared that afternoon together.

A few months later her dad wanted to do something special for her. He managed to get several tickets to Dollywood in Pigeon Forge and asked Taryn to invite some friends to travel to the mountains and spend a day riding the rides, seeing the shows, and then staying overnight in a cabin. Again, she was faced with a dilemma. This time, however, Matt was able to go along. That was one down anyway.

The mention of "road trip" and "free entertainment," not to mention the idea of a hot tub in a cabin, brought out some others. So she and six other people (four girls, two guys) traveled in a caravan to the Smoky Mountains. They'd spent a wonderful day at the theme park and then had the time of their lives in the cabin that night. Someone built a fire and they roasted marshmallows. Matt made a homemade pizza and Taryn drove to Kroger and bought a cheesecake sampler for dessert. She'd fallen asleep with her head in Matt's lap while they all watched a horror movie on television feeling that peaceful, content feeling again.

But after that? Not a word.

"I'm buying friends, Matt," she cried one evening as they sat on her back porch, the light fading from the springtime sky. "I'm basically paying people to spend time with me."

"No you're not," he spoke softly, putting his arm around her shoulders and giving her a hug. "You're just being nice."

"And getting nothing in return. I'm so pathetic. I can't get anyone to do anything with me unless I pay for something," she sniffled into her arm.

"You don't have to pay me. But you can start it you want," he joked.

That was the end of it. She'd gone the rest of her high school years with few friends, but at peace with herself.

The bar was bigger than she'd expected and the parking lot full. She could hear the bass pumping from it as soon as she pulled into the graveled lot. The air was a little chilly so she'd thrown on a light white sweater over her paisley-patterned vintage button down. A few people milled outside, smoking and talking, and their laughter rose over the blues style melody and faded into the night. It was a nondescript place, just a plain old wooden building with one neon sign, but it was out by itself and its isolation gave it an air of cockiness as if saying, "Hey, look at me! I don't need anyone."

When she walked through the doors she was met by a blanket of darkness and a thick, stale scent of cheap draft bear and sweat. Their air was thick, almost pungent, and she knew the cardigan wouldn't last long. She could already feel her armpits dampening. Once her eyes became adjusted, she scanned the tables for Daniel or someone who looked familiar. She found them in a corner in the back, eight of them taking up two round tables. They were far away from the small stage, currently swathed in a bright blue light, and lanterns on their tables framed their faces with a ghostly light.

Taryn wove her way through the swaying dancers on the small dance floor and myriad of tables, sometimes having to turn sideways to squeeze through, until she reached them.

"Hey, there she is," Daniel shouted over the music. He stood up and pulled a chair in next to him and patted it. "Here, sit with me and Willow. Are you drinking?"

Scanning the group she saw a mixture of bottles, drafts, and waters. They seemed to be drinking cheap. "I'll have a coke for now," she smiled. "And maybe work my way up."

"First round's on me then," Daniel laughed. "Gang, if you haven't met Taryn then introduce yourself. Remember, we're paying her so be nice to her and flatter her while I'm gone!"

The rest of them laughed, cast a glance in her direction, and then went back to what they were doing. Two of the guys seemed to be in an intense conversation at the other table. Both of them were waving their hands in the air and occasionally slapping the table or their thighs. They didn't look angry, but she could tell they were talking about something serious. She remembered the one being Jake but she didn't know the other guy.

Willow sat next to her, her long hair pulled back in a French braid. Tonight she was wearing a long black skirt, bright red tank top, and combat boots. Her fingers, which tapped somewhat nervously on the table in front of her, were bedecked in rhinestones. She smiled warmly at Taryn and leaned in to talk to her.

"So Daniel told me about the ghosts. I just wanted to say I think that's pretty awesome."

Taryn had no idea how to reply. "Yeah, well, I think so too when I'm not actually seeing them."

"Do you try talking to them? You know, to see what they want?"

"I've tried. They don't seem to be able to answer the way I hope they will. I don't know they can," Taryn admitted.

"I think they're limited to how they can communicate and they can't exactly, you know…"

"Perform on command?" Willow supplied. "Well, what kind of ghost do you think this one is?"

"It's definitely a woman," Taryn began, feeling just a little silly talking paranormal in a crowded bar with couples dirty dancing to "Blueberry Hill" nearby.

"Oh, yeah," Willow shook her head. "My bad. I meant what type of haunting?"

"Huh?" Now Taryn was confused. "I don't think it's a demon, if that's what you mean."

A look crossed her face making Taryn wonder if Willow thought she was dealing with a moron. "No," she acknowledged patiently, as though talking to a child, "there's actually more than one kind. Let's see if I can put this another way. Okay, sometimes you have ghosts who know they're dead and are kind of floating around, appearing when they think they need to, and communicating with living people. These ghosts might have unfinished business or maybe just don't want to move on. But they definitely know they're dead. Then you have the whole residual energy thing. These aren't really spirits at all. You're just seeing a sign from the past, a scene."

"Like a hologram?" Taryn offered. "I have had this explained to me in the past but I guess I don't understand it."

"Right, like a hologram of sorts," Willow agreed. "The last kind of ghost doesn't know they're dead so they keep living in the same place like they were still alive. These guys need the most help, but it's hard because you can't always communicate with them."

"So where do poltergeists and demons fit in?" Taryn was constantly amazed by the amount of information people seemed to have on this topic. She was new to the whole scene and still learning. Where the heck did THEY learn all this? The Syfy channel? Destination America?

"Those aren't ghosts at all; they're completely different entities. But you don't think that's what your haunting is, right?"

Daniel arrived with the Coke and a Coors for himself. He squeezed in next to Willow and picked up on the conversation he'd overheard while sitting down. "Nah, I don't think it's anything malevolent. Do you, Taryn?"

"No, I don't think so. But it's definitely not the residual thing. Well, some of it is, but not all of it." She still wasn't ready to talk about her camera. "I think she knows she's dead."

"So you *can* communicate with her?" Willow pressed, her eye bright.

"I don't know," Taryn replied helplessly. "I'm trying. But she can get through to me much easier than I can get through to her."

"She must be powerful then," Daniel mused. "To be able to appear to you and try to interact with you. Wonder why she laid dormant all these years?"

"And where she's been," Taryn added. Taking a big swill of her coke she glanced at the other members of the party. "So how's the funding going?"

That got the ear of Joe over at the other table. "Ha," he snorted, "I'm just about finished with the whole thing."

"Why? What's up?"

"The owners called Daniel today. Now they're saying they're going to sell next week. They wanted us off the property, not come around anymore. It was a mess."

"Why?" Taryn asked, shocked. "I'm the only one out there and nobody's bothering anything."

"I don't know," Daniel muttered. "I'm guessing they're getting offered big bucks and someone out there is afraid we're going to have good luck here at the end and get a loan through."

"Am I a problem? I mean, I know that's not the big issue or anything," she added quickly.

"No, no, he got it sorted out," Willow explained. "They don't mind you being there. The woman on the phone was a real bitch, Daniel had it on speaker so I could hear, but by the end she was okay. I guess. They just want all this over with."

"We just need to face the facts," Joe stated, the resignation clearly on his face. "We're not going to get the money, the development company will get it, and a Target or something will go up in its place. We tried; we failed."

The others stopped talking and nodded in agreement.

"And even if we don't," a blond at the end spoke up, "and we actually get it, are people even going to care? Can we keep it up?"

Taryn could see sadness, frustration, and resignation on the groups' faces. "Oh, come on! Don't give up now. You have some time left. And these kinds of things happen all the time. People love museums. With the new interstate exit you can put up brochures at the rest stops, the welcome center. People will stop!" She tried to sound as encouraging as she felt. Nobody's face moved.

"We're just tired," Daniel confessed. Indeed, Delta would have charged him for the bags he carried under his eyes. "And graduation's coming up. Most everyone is going to split. I'm not, and Willow's not, but it means finding new people for the board, new members for the organization. Maybe we just weren't thinking when we took it on as a project."

"I don't believe that," Taryn said stubbornly. "Your hearts were in the right places and that's what counts. If you've turned over all the rocks and haven't found anything then maybe you just need to find a new field."

"We should pay you to be our motivational leader, too," a voice from the end of the table called. Everyone laughed.

The mood lightened then and when Joe offered to buy the next round Taryn let him get her a Jack and Coke. By the third one, she was starting to feel pretty good and wondering if maybe she should reconsider driving back to the B&B.

The group was friendly and made attempts to welcome her. They asked her a few questions about previous jobs, she got into a heated debate with one of the Parks and Recreation majors about the development of the national parks and how much damage some of them had done to the people living in the areas they covered, and she was even asked to dance once. The band played an array of oldies, blues, and classic country. They weren't half bad, even though the longer the night wore on the more out of tune they became. She chalked it up to the pitcher of beer the lead singer kept having refilled.

For a little while she felt relaxed, happy even. The music was loud and the vibrations got under her feet and traveled up her legs. The ratio of Jack to Coke was perfect, not too strong and not too watery, and even though she grew warm, it was a good kind of warm, a cozy kind.

When the band went into some Skynyrd she was pulled up onto the dance floor by everyone else at her table and as she tossed her hair, shook her hips, and waved her arms she experienced a grand feeling of euphoria. Everyone around her laughed and smiled and the bright lights warmed her skin. It was easy to forget she was there for a job, didn't really know these people, and would be leaving soon; she felt a part of them. She was accepted.

Then the band effortlessly slid into "Tuesday's Gone" to continue their tribute to the great southern rockers and those around her paired off. She was left alone on the floor, the disco ball above her leaving spots swirling around her feet. Trying not to feel embarrassed, yet feeling awkward stings on her cheek, she pushed her way between the slow moving bodies and made her way back to the empty table.

There weren't many people sitting down now. The slow ones always got them on their feet. There wasn't much to slow dancing, not really. You just had to turn around in circles and sway your hips a little. Taryn loved to dance, though, or had at one time. She hadn't done it in a long time. That was something from her old life. She and Andrew had frequented country bars when he was alive. He loved the live music as much as she did, but he loved feeling a part of the crowd and excitement even more. Within minutes of walking into a new place he'd meet practically everyone in the room, laughing with the men, flirting with the women...Taryn was never jealous of the attention and admiration Andrew commanded; she was proud of him. Proud to be with him.

But this song...did it have to be so damn long? Did it have to be the one they'd played that night in the kitchen, the night before he died? It was late and she was working in her studio. He wanted a midnight snack and had stuck a Hot Pocket in the microwave. Never one for quiet, he'd cranked up the radio to the classic rock station and then turned it up even louder when Skynyrd came on. She'd wandered into the kitchen then and somehow they wound up dancing in the dark room, giggling because she held onto her Pepsi the whole time.

She didn't remember much of what they did the next day. It was a normal day. But she remembered that night.

Now, sitting there at the table alone, she was struck with a feeling of lonesomeness that hit her like a freight train. She was really and truly by herself, no matter how many people were around her. The punch in her gut was sharp but somehow made her feel as weightless as the feeling of going down that first big hill on a rollercoaster. With a little wave to Daniel out on the dance floor, she let herself out and drove back to her room.

Are you okay?" Matt's voice was groggy, unfocused. She'd woken him up. Of course, it was 2:30 am. Or 22:30 am. It was kind of hard to tell. The numbers kept jumping around. Taryn pulled herself to the edge of the bed to get a closer look at the digital clock and nearly tumbled off onto the floor.

"I'm fine," she slurred. "Just stopped off at the store and picked up some cookies. I had the munchies." Only it came out more like "punchies."

"It sounds like you picked up more than that," Matt said mildly.

Giving up on trying to read the time, Taryn fell back on her pillow and stared up at her ceiling. The ceiling fan was twisting around and around at an impossible speed and now it felt like the whole room was spinning. Bad idea.

"Maybe a little Bailey's," she admitted, glancing at an empty glass on the nightstand to her left. "And a small Jack Daniels," she added, glancing at the empty bottle on the nightstand to her right.

"Well, I hope it was fun." Matt didn't drink; he was a straight arrow. That annoyed the hell out of her.

"I was!" she exclaimed brightly. "I had myself a little party. Only now I'm all out of cookies. And Jack. But I still have some Baileys left..."

If she could just get up and walk to the other side of the room she could remedy that. But the last time she'd tried she'd tripped over her boots and sent herself flying across the floor. She'd made such a racket Delphina had come up to check on her. The look she'd given Taryn was a sad one, but not too judgmental. Taryn was sure she'd seen worse.

"I thought you were going out tonight."

Taryn kicked her feet up in the air, making little circles with her toes. Was one leg longer than the other? Oh God! What was happening to her? Oh, never mind, she sighed with relief. Half her bottom was propped up on a pillow. "I did go out tonight. But I didn't do my drinking there. I *don't* drink and drive."

"Well, that's good," Matt said, relief in his voice.

"Because that's wrong."

"Yes it is."

"And dangerous," she added.

"That's right."

"And it would be nice if you were here in my bed with me."

"What?!" In her drunken state the squeak in his voice sent her into peals of laughter. She muffled them with her blanket, lest Delphina come back up to see what all the racket was again.

"I'm lonely. I didn't realize how lonely I was until tonight. Did you know I haven't slept with anyone since Andrew died?"

"No, I don't believe it's a topic that's ever come up between us," he sighed.

"That's because you're a prude. And I don't mean sex. Because I've done *that*. I mean, I haven't *slept* with anyone, like actually slept. I miss that. I think it's why my nightmares are so bad. There's people around me in motels but it's not the same. It's not like I can just go knock on their doors and ask them if I can get in bed with them," she rambled. She decided to try to make another go of the Baileys and this time she made it all the way across the room to the bottle. Patting herself on the back for this, her triumph was short-lived when she couldn't figure out how to pour the contents into her glass. Finally, she gave up and tilted the bottle back.

"I guess you could but it would be dangerous," he agreed.

"And make me look slutty," she nodded. "'Hey, would you please come and sleep with me?'"

"What?"

"No," Taryn shook her head. "Not *you*. That's what I'd have to say to them."

"Oh."

"Well, I meant that though. *Would* you come and sleep with me? Just crawl in bed with me for a little while? No funny business," she said sternly. Then, on second thought, "Okay, maybe a little funny business."

"This is probably a conversation we should have later," Matt said drily. "When you know what you're saying."

"I'll you know I have exactly what I'm saying," she touted indignantly. "I mean, I'll have you know I know exactly what I'm saying. Oh, you know what I mean. Are you turning me down?"

The Baileys was gone, her Jack was gone, and now she was rooting around the Chips Ahoy package looking for crumbs and stray chocolate pieces.

"Hey, now, I didn't say that," Matt admonished. "I just said we should talk—"

"Because I'm a very good snuggler. And I'm good at other things, too, you know," she declared.

"I'm sure you are."

"Aren't you just a little bit curious?"

"Very; I am *very* curious."

"Hmph." With the last crumb gone she wadded up the package and tossed it across the room in the general direction of the garbage can. "Well, I guess I'll go to sleep now. Good night."

With that, she tossed her phone on her nightstand, stripped down to her bra and underwear, and slithered under the covers. She slept all night with her lamps and television on, but she didn't wake up once.

Chapter 13

When Taryn hobbled down the stairs a little after noon with a queasy stomach and feeling more than a little fragile, she was pleasantly surprised to find Delphina in the kitchen, cooking what smelled like breakfast.

"I heard you walking around upstairs," Delphina called over her shoulder. She was standing at the stove with sizzling sounds emanating from two different skillets. "I thought you might be hungry."

"I'm starved, actually," Taryn admitted, despite the warning rumble in her bowels. She'd spent the past hour in her tiny bathroom. "But you don't have to do this. I can grab something on my way to the tavern."

"I don't mind," Delphina sang. "It's what I enjoy and I wasn't doing anything else. Go find yourself a seat."

Taryn sat down at the dining room table with its starched yellow tablecloth, matching plaid placemats, and salt and pepper shakers shaped like lighthouses. A plate of toast, apple butter and jelly on the side, was already waiting for her.

She'd managed to scarf down two pieces by the time Delphina brought the scrambled eggs, English muffin, sausage, and fried potatoes in. "Geeze," she laughed. "You went to a lot of trouble."

"No real trouble," Delphina shrugged her small shoulders. "I had a difficult night myself. This kept me busy today and took my mind off things."

"I'm not usually like that," Taryn said after a few bites.

"Like what, dear?" Delphina was busying herself around the room with the pretense of sweeping and dusting but it appeared to Taryn as though she was simply going through the motions.

"Drunk."

"Oh, that," Delphina waved her hand in the air, her assortment of rings sparkling in the sunlight. "A little silliness from time to time is good for the soul."

"I'm sorry."

"I imagine you had a lot on your mind for you to think you needed to do it."

Taryn nodded. "I guess I did. I guess I feel lonely."

"It's hard, isn't it?" Delphina sighed. "Being a strong woman and then admitting that, as much as you'd like to, you really can't do everything on your own."

"Yes, it's hard," Taryn agreed. "I think I'm going to make some changes, though."

She'd spent all morning, in between bouts of visiting the bathroom and lying back down on the bed to stare at Investigation Discovery (a marathon of missing people episodes) and had made an executive decision: She was going to call Jamie. She'd nearly forgotten about him but while cleaning out her jean pockets that morning his card fell out and she'd stared at the number for a long time. And why not call him? She could dig up more dirt, go horseback riding, and talk to someone. She was too embarrassed to call Matt, despite the fact he'd texted her three times that morning, and Daniel & Co. had their own things going on. Jamie was neutral. It was time she took another step in that direction anyway.

She called Jamie on the way to the tavern. If he was surprised to hear from her he didn't show it. He did, however, sound happy which was a boost to her ego. She even laughed a few times on the phone, despite the fact her head and stomach were still soft. They agreed to meet on Friday. By the time she hung up the phone she was feeling quite a bit better so when she turned up the radio and heard "Glory Days" she cranked it up even louder and sang along in her off-key, flat voice. She *would* make this a good day. She had to. Enough of sitting around, feeling sorry for herself.

The sky was gloomy and slate-colored with the threat of rain by the time she reached the tavern. The breeze was still faint, though, and since there weren't any sprinkles yet she set up her easel and got to work. She could always hightail it out of there in a hurry if it came down to it. She felt guilty, anyway, for getting such a late start.

"Sorry, dude," she murmured to the canvas as she touched it with her brush. "I've been neglecting you." And she was. She should've been a lot further along. She'd have to pull a few all-nighters and work in her room to get it completed on time. This playing Nancy Drew bit was getting in the way of her work. As a professional, she was embarrassed by this. She was always invested in her paintings, and in the houses and structures she worked with, but never to this extent. Now she was more concerned with

198

solving a mystery (a mystery that might not even exist since she was the only one seeing anything) than doing her job. That *had* to stop. She needed to finish up, move on, and find something else. The tavern would go on without her. Or it wouldn't. Either way, it shouldn't be her concern.

Of course, it would break her heart if it got torn down.

When the first big splatters of rain landed on her head she quickly threw a sheet of plastic over her paints and moved her canvas to the car, protecting it first before going back to collect the paints, along with her easel and brushes.

By the time she loaded the last of it in the trunk the rain was coming down in torrents. Her feet were wet and muddy, thanks to her sandals, and she could barely see through her dripping hair that hung in chunks around her face. She'd have to peel her jeans off; they were plastered to her body. It was a cold rain, too, and chilled her to the bone. She was looking forward to getting back to her room, drying off, and curling up in the bed and watching more trashy TV for the rest of the day. But she was also glad she'd dragged herself out and worked, even if it was only for an hour.

Taryn was all the way in the car with the engine on and her foot on the brake when she noticed the glittering in a downstairs window of the tavern. At first she thought it was a trick of the light, or maybe even a brief flash of lightning, but when it happened a second time she knew it wasn't. It was a light, a faint one, and it was slowly moving back and forth. Squinting her eyes, she peered forward and tried to see clearly through the rain drops. Was it a flashlight? Was someone in there? She didn't think so. There weren't any cars around and unless someone had parked very far away and walked, which was possible, she didn't know where they would've come from. She'd been there for at least an hour and hadn't seen anyone coming or going.

Against what she knew was her better judgment, she turned the engine off, pocketed the keys, and trudged back out in the wet towards the tavern.

Fog was beginning to close in now, creating a barrier between the property and the highway. She could almost imagine she was isolated, shut off from the rest of the world. Inside the house, the only sound resonating through the walls was the splash of rain against the windows and what was left of the roof. It smelled damp, a different kind of scent than what she was used to there. Normally, the tavern carried a dry, dusty scent. She worried if something didn't happen soon, the whole building was going to collapse. Then she remembered that if something didn't happen soon the whole building was just going to be torn down anyway. A little rain wouldn't make a difference.

The overcast skies made the house even darker than usual, but she'd brought her flashlight back with her. With the added light she was able to examine the multiple layers of wallpaper in the parlor (six, as far as she could count) and see the scuffs on the floors a little better (left over from boots a century before or from moving furniture ten years ago, she couldn't be sure) but with the house devoid of furniture there wasn't much to poke around in.

She tried reasoning with the walls as she walked around them. "You're going to have to give me a little more to work with," she sighed in Permelia's room. "I'm kind of starting to think this is all in my head or you're just haunting me. Maybe you ARE just a regular old, pardon the word dear, ghost and I've made this out to be much more than it is. But I feel like you want something. If you didn't, then why do you keep bothering me?"

The house was silent. She took a few experimental shots with Miss Dixie, but the images came back ordinary. There may have been an orb in one of them, or perhaps it was just dust; she couldn't be sure. There definitely wasn't some ghostly image of a woman emerging from a wardrobe, bed, or any other piece of furniture no longer there.

"Can we make a deal then?" she continued as she started back down the stairs. "If you don't need anything can you just back off a little bit? I wouldn't mind sleeping or not feeling like someone or something was staring at me every few minutes. A girl's gotta have some privacy, you–"

The words were barely out of her mouth when a force so powerful she'd have bruises later shoved her and sent her flying. She was only two stairs from the ground, but the floor reached out to her at such a dizzying speed she was sure she'd sink right through it. With a shriek she flipped Miss Dixie over her shoulder and braced for impact. When she hit with a "thud" her right forearm grazed the rough pine floors and her legs twisted at an awkward angle under her. She lay there for a second, feeling blood starting to ooze out of her arm, and gently stretched her legs to make sure nothing was broken or sprained. Since she could wiggle her toes, she assumed everything was okay. But, damn it, she was going to be in pain tomorrow.

"Now what the hell was *that*?" she muttered, attempting to scramble to her feet. She was afraid to look behind her, afraid the set of eyes she could feel would turn out to be real and attached to something hideous and unimaginable.

Slowly, the wall next to her began to shudder. It was gentle at first and then made a grumbling noise as though it hadn't been fed in a very long time. On her hands and knees, she backed up to the wall behind her and felt her way to safety, ignoring the pain in her arm and legs. The bead board trembled and then, with what sounded like a long sigh of frustration, popped. The wall opened.

Only, it wasn't a wall. It was a door.

The door was tiny, only about two feet high. There was no handle. It was carved so perfectly into the wall it was no wonder she'd missed it. Taryn covered her eyes with her scraped hands and held her breath, certain something would jump out at her or try to drag her in. She'd seen far too many horror movies that had done the very same. Unfortunately, she was too terrified to actually move and run, turning her into one of those big-breasted bimbos who are constantly running up the stairs when they should be running out the back door.

When a few seconds went by without any further action, however, she opened her fingers and peered through them. Aside from it being deathly quiet (she couldn't even hear the rain anymore) she saw nothing menacing. She was simply sitting at the bottom of an old staircase, with a small door open in front of her that probably hadn't been undone in years.

Still not completely at ease, she removed her flashlight and aimed its beam at the entrance. The door wasn't open wide enough to see all the way inside so she stretched out her foot and gave it a kick, ready to spring up and run if anything (dead or otherwise) came out at her. It opened with a deliberate moan that made her jump a little, but when nothing else happened she released a sigh of relief.

With her flashlight she was able to see three of the walls. It wasn't a big room, she calculated; maybe three feet by three feet at most. Just a storage room. It was dark and dusty, but empty. With slightly more courage now, she waddled towards it on a crouch and peered inside. There were a few ugly looking spiders and an old boot but the room was otherwise vacant. No dead bodies, no vagrant hiding out and ready to pounce on her, no pot of gold.

Taryn was disappointed.

Standing up and dusting her jeans off, she gave the little door a slight push and looked back up the stairs. On the stair she'd tripped on she saw a small stick. Maybe she'd tripped on it. And the vibration had caused the door to open. She was losing her mind. There wasn't anything paranormal here at all.

Taryn's phone made the "dun dun dun" of "Law and Order," signifying a text from Matt. She'd been avoiding his calls and texts all day. Still embarrassed from her drunken phone call the night before, she still wasn't ready to explain herself and was too uncomfortable to pretend like she hadn't said anything at all. Matt wasn't a drinker, except for the occasional glass of wine at supper, and he'd never known the thrill, and sometimes later mortification, of being drunk and letting your tongue run loose. Matt liked to be in control of his words and thoughts at all times. Intoxication was one of his worst fears. Taryn felt that was kind of a shame. Some of the fondest times she couldn't remember involved alcohol.

Sinking into the bubble bath, though, and loosening up a bit after the dampness and disappointment of most of the day helped. She had to answer him back. He wouldn't give up.

Slipping her hand out of the water, she dried it off and read what he wrote: "Me and Charlie Talkin.'"

With a laugh bubbling in her throat, she laid the phone back down on a towel and closed her eyes, trying to think of an adequate response. When all else failed, they used songs to communicate with one another. This one, by Miranda Lambert, was about a boy and girl who met at a young age and started up a puppy love. She and Matt met when they were children; she didn't know about treating their love like fireflies but they'd certainly caught enough together. It was just another reminder that their friendship went back a long ways. It was no good to ignore it or him.

Biting her lip, she picked her phone up and typed back: "Feed Jake."

A few seconds later, the phone rang. Before she had the chance to say anything Matt snorted, "Either you're comparing me to a dog or you're putting an imaginary one above me."

"I thought you liked that song. And the video was about two guys who were friends all their lives," she pointed out.

"You know I didn't have cable until I was a teenager."

"Good point," she conceded. "But still, it's never wrong to bring up Pirates of the Mississippi."

"So...you drunk called me last night and now you're too embarrassed to talk to me, right?"

Chewing on her lip she stared at the tiles on the bathroom wall. Delphina, or someone, had taken the time to hand stamp all of them with purple irises. It was pretty. Made her miss having a place she could decorate. "Yes, I guess so. Sorry about that."

"Don't worry about it. You've said worse."

It was true.

"Besides," he said, seriously for him, "I enjoyed it."

Well, *that* was different.

"I'll have to do it again sometime. I aim to please," she replied cheerfully.

"So do I, Taryn. You have no idea."

Now it was her turn to blush. Moving right along..."I was at the tavern today. Something pushed me down the stairs. Or else I tripped. It's hard to say. I thought something pushed me at first but then I found this stick...Anyway. A door opened to this little room, but it was empty."

"Maybe something used to be in there," he suggested. "Maybe you were supposed to see it anyway."

"Maybe," she agreed. "And maybe I've just been watching too much 'Criminal Minds.' You know they show, like, twenty episodes back to back on some channels at night. It might be messing with me. When the door opened I expected to find some sadist's lair, complete with acid vats or something."

"Well, I'm glad you didn't."

"You and me both," she snorted.

"Are you giving up on the paranormal angle?"

"Maybe," she conceded. "I know I'm seeing Permelia. I know she's hanging around me. But maybe there isn't really anything for me to 'solve.' Maybe it's just...I don't know. A control thing."

"Come again?"

"No, seriously, I've been thinking about this a lot," she explained. "Maybe I think I need to solve something, need to fix something, because I don't feel in control of what's happening in my life. I don't know. It made sense at the time," she finished lamely.

"Just keep hanging in there," Matt advised. "You'll figure it out. You always do."

Chapter 14

*H*e usually worked on Fridays, Jamie told her, but

he was due for some time off. She felt guilty for the fact he
was making accommodations for her, but she couldn't help
but feel flattered. He looked different than he had at the
Frosty Freeze; then, he'd been wearing tattered jeans, a
stained T-shirt, and mud-crusted work boots. Today he was
wearing a red flannel shirt rolled up at the sleeves, dark

pants, snakeskin cowboy boots, and a Dallas Cowboys baseball cap. He was clean shaven and his blond hair was thick and wavy. He reminded her a little bit of Cary Elwes (more "The Princess Bride" than "Saw"). He was waiting in the parking lot when she pulled up to the stables and his mouth widened in a huge smile when he saw her.

Taryn was nervous when she got out of the car and walked towards him but he instantly put her at ease as he began telling her about the stables and his history with riding. It was only the second time they'd met, but she already felt like he was an old friend.

"So when's the last time you rode?" he asked, leading her to the horses. She liked that he got right down to business. He'd already gotten a horse ready for her, but told her she could wipe hers down and feed her when they were finished if she wanted.

"A long time," she admitted. "I rode as a kid, took lessons. Then we later had friends with horses. When I was home for an extended period of time we'd go over and ride." She didn't elaborate on the "we." It was too early in the day to bring up an ex-husband, much less a dead one.

"Well, I give lessons and train," he explained, gesturing to a handful of children in one of the riding rings. "I think riding a horse is a lot like riding a bike. You never really forget how."

Her mare was a gentle Appaloosa with big eyes and a sweet disposition. After spending a few minutes stroking her and saying her hellos, Taryn mounted her, excited at the prospect of spending the day outdoors doing something besides working. Jamie was easygoing, friendly, and didn't seem to be pushing her into anything. She could just have easily been with a girlfriend—a very good-looking male one, that is. And one with an excellent behind.

"It's a little crowded today since the weather is nice so we won't stick to the usual trails," he explained as they started out of the stable. "There's one we let the advanced riders go on, and that the staff uses. Nobody will be on it today. I thought you might enjoy something more private. It's up to you, of course."

He had a dazzling smile when he directed it at her. "Since I haven't done this in a long time I think the fewer people I have the potential to trample the better."

The path was lined with trees and dappled with sunlight. The air smelled sweet and crisp, like autumn. She'd worn a blue flannel shirt and jeans and it was just enough to keep her from feeling cold. They rode next to each other, his Tennessee Walker's coat glossy in the sun shine. He rode very well and moved with his horse in a rhythm she might have even called sexy. Despite his big hands, height (she guessed him over six feet), and strong arms and shoulders he handled his horse with a loving gentleness. She'd seen the way Jamie'd slipped him a sugar cube and kissed him on the nose before he mounted.

"So how's the job?" Jamie asked conversationally. "How do you like working at the tavern?"

She knew he didn't mean the ghost and Permelia and was just inquiring about her painting. "It's an interesting place, to say the least," she laughed. "But I like it. I love all my jobs. I have the luxury now of being able to pick the ones that draw me the most."

"That must be nice," he replied. "To be able to do something you love, I mean. So...what exactly do you do?"

"Well, for all intents and purposes I'm an artist. Multi-media, actually, although most clients hire me for my painting. My photography is just for fun, just for me. I get called into places on the verge of demolition, mostly, and I do paintings of them to show what they would've looked like in their prime. There's usually a lot of reconstruction in my work. I don't paint them the way they look now; I show what they would have looked like in the past."

He nodded in understanding. "So do you also get called in to work with architects, too, then? For renderings?"

The familiar ache pulled at her as she thought of Andrew, the architect. That's exactly what the two of them did together–he made the plans and came up with the ideas and she drew them. "Not so much anymore, although that is basically what I'm doing with this job."

"Word around town is those kids are trying to get the money to buy it," he said as he steered her deeper into the woods. It was darker here, and quieter.

"They are. But they've hit a few roadblocks. One of their grants was denied. They've had trouble raising money." She felt a little disloyal revealing their financial problems, even though they weren't top secret.

"I know the owner. He's pretty hard up for cash. He's a nice guy, but worried. I know he wants to sell," Jamie offered.

"Yes, but he wants to sell sooner than they'll be able to buy, I'm afraid," Taryn said with regret. "I hate to see the place torn down."

"Me too," Jamie agreed. "I'm into those old buildings. You know—houses, barns...old stores. Sometimes I like to go out for aimless drives and take pictures of them when the weather's nice."

"You do?" Taryn beamed with pleasure. "That's one of my favorite things to do. It's how I got started, actually."

"I belong to a few online groups," Jamie grinned. "Urban exploring. A few Facebook groups. You know, Deserted Places, Abandoned Places, sites like that. We upload pictures and talk about them."

"I belong to a few myself. I may have commented on some of your pictures and didn't know it," Taryn laughed.

They continued to ride on in companionable silence. Taryn was enjoying herself much more than she'd expected. It was easy being out with him; she was comfortable in her skin. That rarely happened with new people, it generally took her awhile to warm up, but with Jamie she didn't find herself measuring what she said or how she said it. The pressure of being on a date wore off, probably because he wasn't treating it like one. She was grateful for that.

When they neared a small creek Jamie led the horses to a thick oak tree and swung out of his saddle with ease. He first tied up his horse and then helped her down by grabbing her around the waist and swinging her to the ground in one fluid movement. Her heart fluttered a little and she blushed, hoping he didn't notice.

"I brought a snack," he explained, producing a battered knapsack decorated with sew-on patches of state parks. "It's not exactly a lunch, but it will boost our energy. I hope you like sandwiches, cookies, and apple juice."

The apple juice charmed her. "Never met a cookie I didn't like," she said. "Well, except ones with raisins. Not because I don't like raisins, but because I always think they're going to be chocolate chip."

"And then you're disappointed when you bite into them?" he questioned knowingly. She nodded. "I get that. No raisins here. Just good old chocolate chip and white chocolate macadamia nut."

For the next half hour they lounged by the creek, talking a little and enjoying one another's company. She didn't feel pressed to constantly keep up a conversation and apparently he didn't either and they occasionally lapsed into easy silence. He brought out his camera a few times and took shots of the water, and of her, and that won her over even more.

"So what's your story?" she asked after awhile. "Why aren't you married or something? Or *are* you?"

Dusting cookie crumbs off his hands he chuckled, the tips of his ears turning a little red. "Well, to be honest, I was engaged once. That was three years ago. When it ended I never got enthused about dating again. I go out sometimes, mostly just to be social, but I prefer my own company just as much. Except with you, of course," he added quickly.

"What happened to your engagement, if you don't mind my asking?"

Jamie sighed and gazed at the water. She was afraid she'd put her foot in her mouth and was about to tell him not to worry about it when he began talking. "She was a sweet woman; I'd known her since high school. Wouldn't have hurt a fly. We were very good friends as well as partners. Unfortunately, she got mixed up with some wrong people. Got into prescription pain pills at first and later meth. It's a nasty habit; dangerous. I couldn't stand what it was doing to her. I talked her into rehab once and she tried." Exhaling sharply, he picked up a small stick and threw it into the water, watched it bob and float a few feet before continuing. "It wasn't enough. Maybe I'm weak but I just couldn't watch her tear herself apart like that. Her hair fell out, her skin...she looked like she was fifteen years older than she was. And she changed. Her personality, that is. The reminder of what she used to be compared to what she became was too much."

"I'm sorry," Taryn said sincerely. It sounded terrible. "And you definitely weren't weak for not sticking it out. At the end of the day, it's your life too. So what happened to her?"

"She eventually got herself sorted out. But it's a lifelong process. She met someone at one of her meetings. I think she's happy. I hope so. It happens a lot around here, though. These interstate towns, they're getting hit hard from what I hear. Runners going between the big cities. I think it's an epidemic. But anyway..." He shrugged and threw another stick into the water, watched it ripple. "What about you? A jealous boyfriend or husband I should know about?" he teased.

And now was when things became even less lighthearted, if that was possible. She briefly told him about Andrew. And watched while his face turned serious. "Geeze, I'm sorry Taryn. That's awful. And he was so young."

"I worked with him, too," she explained. "He was an architect. We met on a job. We did a lot of jobs together after we started dating. Almost exclusively worked together once we got married. It was more than just losing my husband and best friend; I lost my business partner, too."

"You're so young to have been through that," he said sadly, handing her a cookie. "Cookie?"

She smiled and accepted it. "It feels like a lifetime ago. And yesterday."

A little while later they untied their horses and began their journey back to the stables. It was late afternoon and the crowd had picked up.

After wiping down her horse she waited for Jamie while he put everything away and washed off. She watched from a distance as others approached him, shook his hand, slapped him on the back, spoke to him. He was well-liked, she could tell.

He walked her back to the parking lot, his hands stuffed in his pockets. "Listen, I had a great time today," he began before they reached her car. "If it's okay, I'd like to do this again. Maybe not riding, of course, although we can do that if you want."

"I'd like to see you again, too," she agreed. "I could use a friend. I'll be in town a few more weeks. I'm staying at the B&B." She gave him her cell number.

When they reached her car door, he opened it for her. Before she got in, he laid his hand on her shoulder. "I wanted to tell you I don't normally try to schedule the second date before I'm off the first one," he said shyly. Now, at the end of the day, she liked the fact he was thinking of their time as a "date." "I'm just afraid someone else might snatch you up so I feel like I should jump in here fast."

Taryn flushed with pleasure and bit her lip in shyness. Up close, he was incredibly handsome. His eyes were a piercing blue with just the faintest hint of brown around them. Even though he'd been riding all day, he smelled fresh and rustic, like a tree. Manly. "I think that sounds nice. Just call me, okay?"

He leaned over and quickly kissed her on the cheek, something she found delightful. She appreciated the fact he wasn't trying to move in on her or do anything too quickly. As she drove away, he stood in place and watched her, throwing up his hand in a wave.

I know his parents," Delphina stated, her lips pursed in concentration. "A very nice, respectable young man."

This morning Delphina was dressed in purple polyester slacks and a white pullover with small irises blooming down the front. Her hair was pinned and sprayed in place; she looked very prim and proper (albeit, colorful). Taryn was in her bathrobe.

"We had a very nice time," Taryn said, digging into her stack of blueberry pancakes. "I'd forgotten how much I enjoy riding. I'm going to see him again. He asked me before I left."

"So he's intelligent, too," Delphina nodded. "Good. A smart man doesn't let a good woman get away."

Taryn's phone rang and she excused herself. It was 8:00 am on a Saturday and Daniel was calling, something that hadn't happened before.

"Daniel?" she answered, a little confused. "Everything okay?"

"No, it's not." His voice was hard, bitter.

"What's up? Am I fired?" she joked.

"It's not you," he seethed. "You know the Kickstarter campaign Joe started?"

"Yeah. I looked at it myself and sent it around to some friends. What's the matter?"

"We were up almost $6,000. Not a lot, I know, but it was a good start. Today three of the backers pulled out. Almost half of the money. No reason. They just quit."

"Well that's weird," she mused. "What do you think happened?"

"I don't know," he sputtered in exasperation. "Two of the guys own businesses here in town. One's a chiropractor and one has a tree removal service. The other is a professor of mine. I'm going to go talk to them, see what's up."

"I don't blame you for being upset," she cajoled, trying to calm him down although she was nearly as upset as him. "But remember, when you speak to them, be professional. Don't let them see you upset."

"Yeah, I know," he said sullenly. "It just makes me so mad. And disappointed. We hit walls everywhere we turn, it feels like."

"How's the grant coming along?"

"We hope to hear something on Monday. Also applied for some loans, too. They're not much but, well, you know. We're hoping if we can get at least some cash together maybe the owner will work with us."

It was a longshot, especially considering what she was sure the development company was offering, but at least they were trying. That was the important thing.

"I'm going to go on out there later this afternoon. If you want to talk you know where I'll be."

The conversation left her heated and frustrated. The kids were *trying*, that was more than most people did, yet their actions felt fruitless. She was disappointed *for* them.

When Delphina came back into the room, Taryn was pacing, her pancakes forgotten. "Everything okay, dear?"

"Just some problems with funding," she explained. "Some backers pulled their money out and didn't give a reason. I almost feel like someone is trying to sabotage their efforts."

"It's always a money issue. I wish we could go back to bartering," Delphina muttered.

"You and me both," Taryn agreed.

She was finished eating but now she sat back down in her chair, trying to summon up the courage to ask Delphina what was on her mind. Finally, she just took a deep breath and went for it. "Listen, I wanted to ask you something, but I don't want to sound crazy."

"I highly doubt you could do that," Delphina smiled. "What's wrong?"

"Have you, um, ever seen a ghost here? Or felt anything? Heard anything?"

Delphina studied her, considering, and then shook her head. "No," she replied a little sadly. "I haven't. It's just me here. Sometimes I think if this place was haunted then at least I'd have a little company."

............His hands were rough against her skin, their calluses scraping the delicate curve of her hips. She fought him like a wild animal as he clawed at her breasts and tore the fabric from her, the thick cotton shredding like silk. The room was so dark she could barely make out his features, but she knew who he was; he'd been watching her all night downstairs. Had grabbed at her once as she walked by. If only she'd told James...

The whiskey on his breath was sour. The acrid scent filled her nostrils and made her stomach churn until she could feel the bile rose in her throat. It would serve him right if she was sick on him, she thought as she scratched at his eyes, his nose, whatever she could grab ahold of.

The drink didn't make him any weaker. He might have been intoxicated, but he still outweighed her and his large frame crushed her tiny body. She attempted to scream as he tugged his trousers down and she felt his pulsating manhood against her naked thigh, but he pushed the blanket around her face until she gagged on it, unable now to catch her breath at all. The music and laughter downstairs was loud, vibrating the walls as she thrashed against him. She was only a few feet from those who might save her but none knew she struggled.

With lightning-quick speed he sought her tender entrance and pressed forward. Refusing to quit fighting, she tossed from side to side, kicking her legs with all her strength and bucking as he laughed in her face, his breath a putrid cloud of poison. She might die, but she wouldn't go down easily.

Then, she felt a weakness. The drink might not have hurt his strength, but it did hurt other things. Try as he might, he was unable to enter her. Just when she thought she might die from lack of air, he moved his hands from her face and the blanket as he tried to guide himself forward. She could feel him, soft and wilted, against her tight muscles. He used his rough fingers to push and tear her and blood seeped from her wound but he was still unable to do what he sought.

Using this as an opportunity, despite her fear and pain, she rammed her fists at his chest and face, almost *throwing to him to the floor. Now, though, he'd lost interest in her nether regions. If he couldn't have her there, he'd find another outlet for his energy.*

With a startling force he slapped her across the face. The act left her stunned; she saw stars, even in the darkness. Her gasp drove him forward like a moan of pleasure might. Using his fists now, he pummeled and pounded her chest, her head, her stomach, and her arms until she finally slipped into blackness.

Taryn woke up thrashing and moaning, her face wet with tears, acid in her throat. Her blankets were in a disheveled heap on the floor and her pillow was across the room where she must have thrown it. As soon as she realized she was awake she jumped out of bed and threw on the light. Standing in the middle of her modern bedroom, alone, with her arms out in front of her still in defense mode it was hard to believe that just moments ago she was fighting off an invisible attacker that felt so real she could still feel his fists and smell the liquor on his breath. Her heart was racing, the adrenalin so strong she felt like she could've easily ran a mile.

Nobody had ever forced Taryn into sex before; she'd never known anything but gentleness and kindness in that act. But she'd felt him trying to push into her, felt her own muscles fight against him, felt herself ripping. It was a primal violation that left her angered and frightened and even a little guilty, although she knew she hadn't done anything wrong. At the edge of these feelings was the ghost of embarrassment, too. Something like that didn't happen to her, wasn't supposed to.

But it was just a dream. Just a dream, she reminded herself.

Still trembling, she made her way to her bed and turned on the television. A rerun of "The Brady Bunch" was playing, the episode with Davy Jones on. Taryn turned up the volume and unsteadily climbed back into bed and picked up her phone.

To Matt: "Blind and Afraid of the Dark."

A few moments later, the "Law and Order" tone. To Taryn: "Every Light in the House is On."

Chapter 15

*T*aryn stepped out of the abandoned school

clutching Miss Dixie in hand, beaming from ear to ear. "That was amazing," she breathed happily. "The desks are still in there! How long has it been closed?"

"About ten years," Jamie answered, closing the door firmly behind him. "They closed it when they built the new one across town. This one was built with WPA money. It was dated. I still love it, though. I went to school here."

They began walking back to Jamie's truck, Taryn stopping every few feet to turn and stare at the two story brick building behind them. "The newer schools are modern, sterile. They might be better, but they lack character. I mean, the entrance alone is worth salvaging."

"I love all the woodwork in these older places," Jamie agreed. "The floors, the tall doors, the details. They don't build them like they used to."

He'd promised to take her exploring and he had. The old ivy-covered school had a caved in roof from a tornado the year before and extensive water damage, but Taryn looked past that. Instead, she heard the laughter of children, the running of feet down the hallways, locker doors slamming. She could still hear basketballs pounding the floors in the gym, doors banging, and the bell signaling the start and end of the day.

"You hungry?" he asked once they were in his truck.

"I could eat."

Once they were seated in the small café in town they went through some of her pictures, Jamie telling her more stories about the school and some of the antics he'd gotten into as an elementary student. Taryn found herself laughing and enjoying herself again. The bad dream she'd had a few nights ago still weighed heavy on her mind but it was good to focus on other things. That's why she was glad when he called her and asked her out again.

"So what's going on with the project?"

"They lost some money," she sighed, biting into her pepper jack burger. "I don't know why. Daniel was supposed to go talk to some of the donors and sort it out. I haven't heard anything yet."

"So if they don't raise the money..."

"They don't get the tavern. I want to help them, but I'm almost finished with the painting and I don't know where to go from here."

"Do you think they can earn it?" She liked the fact he was so interested. Having someone to talk to about her work was fun. Matt was so used to what she did he rarely expressed interest in it, although he was always willing to listen if she needed to get something off her chest.

"I honestly don't know. Stranger things have happened. There's a lot of people out there who want to help projects like these. If their campaign got in the right hands...maybe."

They continued eating in silence, Taryn lost in her thoughts. She'd contacted Eve and introduced herself. She hadn't heard back from her yet but she was hopeful. She was placing a big amount of importance on what the letters might say.

"You look like you have something on your mind," Jamie said at last. "Anything you want to talk about?"

"Nothing important I guess," she shrugged, trying to smile brightly. "Just some other things going on."

"Like what? I'm all ears."

"You'd think I was cracked if I told you."

"I don't know, Taryn; try me." He looked so earnest with his serious eyes and soft smile she couldn't help but want to talk to him. But it was only their second date. She didn't want to scare him off. Still, the chance their relationship would even go anywhere was very slim anyway. The job would end, she'd move on, and they'd lose touch. That's just the way things happened.

"Okay." She set down her sandwich and took a big drink of Pepsi. "Do you believe in ghosts?"

"Yes, absolutely."

"Just like that?"

"Well," he said thoughtfully, "I don't believe everyone who thinks they had a paranormal experience actually had one, but I do believe ghosts exist."

"How can you be so sure?"

"I believe in a god," he shrugged. "I believe in a higher power, in an afterlife, in a soul. A ghost just seems to fit right in there. Maybe it's leftover energy, maybe it's just a memory, or maybe it IS the spirit of a person who has passed on. But I can't believe in a higher power without believing the body has a soul. And if I believe in a soul, I don't see it being that big of a stretch to think the soul can travel."

"That's a very good answer. I am not religious at all. I don't even know what I believe. I believe in something, but I can't put it into words. I'm not very good at that. But I believe in ghosts. I see them."

"As in you see dead people?" he smiled at her, but he wasn't making fun.

"Okay, here's the thing. I'm not one of these people who think they have a special power and nobody else can do what they do," she explained. "I think ghosts exist and everyone has the capacity to see and hear them. Maybe some people are more tuned in than others; maybe some people explain them away and don't give them credit for what they are. I don't know. What I can do, though, is see them in a way I've never known anyone else to."

She briefly gave him a rundown on Miss Dixie and her capacity to see the dead, and their belongings, through her camera.

"That's amazing," Jamie said when she finished. "It's almost like your camera allows you to time travel. Is it just *that* camera?"

"No, but I wondered that myself. The thing is, it was just the camera, with the occasional weird feelings and stuff. Now, though, it seems to be getting stronger. I'm seeing and hearing a lot of things outside the camera. And, I know this sounds weird, I think I'm even being visited in my dreams."

"That doesn't surprise me," he murmured. "It seems like something you could develop, make it stronger. And that's what you're doing, even if it's unintentional."

"It just started all of a sudden. Just a few months ago, out of the blue."

"Now *that* I'm not sure I believe," he laughed.

"What do you mean?"

"Well, how long have you loved old buildings? Loved exploring? Been into urbex?"

She tapped her fingers on the table, considering. "All my life, really. When I was a kid I used to love the movies with the old houses. And as a teenager mine and my friend's idea of fun was to drive around and look at them and explore when we could. Later, I made a degree out of it in college.

But nothing paranormal ever happened in them. Well, except for when I was a little kid. But that wasn't an old house."

"Maybe you're looking at it all wrong," he suggested. "Have you ever thought perhaps you were drawn to these interests because of something inside you? That it was your ability to feel for the buildings and the stories making you interested in them? Maybe you couldn't actually see the people and their possessions plainly like you do now, but you've always felt them. You just didn't know what that feeling was."

The idea was a good one, and even a little frightening. When she'd looked at empty rooms in the past and saw them filled with furniture in her mind, she'd always thought she just had a big imagination. But what if it hadn't been her imagination at all? What if back then she was actually feeling things she was now seeing?

"When I was little," she whispered, "I had a bad night. I was staying with my grandmother. I crawled up into her bed and buried my head in her arm. She whispered something to me that night. It made me feel...better. More secure."

"What did she say?" Jamie whispered back, his eyes focused on her.

"For the longest time I couldn't remember. It was like I'd blocked it out. But then I was in the hospital over the summer and it came to me. Just out of the blue. She said, 'This is all for you. You're here for a reason.'"

"That comforted you?"

"Yes," Taryn nodded. "I didn't feel defenseless anymore. I felt empowered, important. I think maybe I've carried that with me, even though I couldn't exactly remember the words."

"My grandmother taught me to play poker," he stated, twitching his lips.

They both broke out into peals of laughter.

You did what?" Matt demanded.

"I actually kissed a man," Taryn laughed, doing a little twirl in her bedroom. She felt like a teenager. "It's the first real kiss I've had in years. I thought it was going to be strange, but it wasn't. You would approve; he was a complete gentleman."

Matt was silent.

"Oh, come on. Don't you want me to get back on the horse?"

"Do you have to be crude about it?" he complained.

"Oh, you're taking me too literally. We're not going to go jump in the sack...yet."

"You would do that?" he asked, appalled.

"I am an adult, Matt," she replied. "What's wrong with sleeping someone you like and are attracted to?"

"There is no good reason for you to do it," he muttered.

"Oh, there's plenty of reasons for me to do it. And good ones, too. But I don't need to justify it. I can do it simply because I want to. And what are you, my dad?" she demanded.

"I just don't know if I can talk to you right now," he seethed. "This upsets me."

"Matt!" She was honestly shocked at his behavior. "We're not teenagers. And you do realize we're talking about hypothetical sex don't you? We haven't even planned the next date yet."

"Just tell me about your work," he said at last, changing the subject.

She hung up the phone feeling bad. She'd suspected Matt had a thing for her over the years but neither one of them had ever acted upon it, not even when they'd had the chance. There was a time in high school when they'd exchanged some love letters and she'd sworn she was completely in love with him, but she was thirteen at the time.

He'd never made a real move on her and, months later, when she met Andy Moody (the new kid from New Jersey) she's fallen head over heels for him and that was the end of that.

Of course, there was the time when she was twenty-one and they'd shared the Christmas Eve kiss. She couldn't forget that. It was snowing, the first snow she'd seen in a long time. She and Matt had celebrated Christmas Eve at the Opryland Hotel in Nashville. They'd seen a show and then gone to dinner at the hotel. It was late when they got out and they pretty much had the atriums to themselves as they walked around. She was wearing tall high heels and her feet had been killing her. She held on first to his arm and then to his hand as he supported her around the hotel. He kept insisting they leave so she could rest her feet, but she loved the hotel, especially at Christmas, and she didn't want to waste it that night. It was beautiful with its Christmas lights sparkling through the trees like fireflies, the soft holiday music playing, and the bubbling indoor stream.

She'd finally allowed him to move her to a bench. It was secluded, hidden by trees and poinsettia arrangements. Nobody bothered them or even walked by. Above them, in rooms with balconies overlooking the atrium, she could see television sets playing and people tucked away in their rooms. But she felt as though they were alone.

At first he had simply bent forward and rested his forehead on hers. They'd laughed then because the curve of her nose perfectly cradled his forehead, as though their faces were made for one another. They'd stayed like that for a second, only inches apart. She could feel his warm breath on her cheeks, on her lips. Then she'd reached up and touched the back of his head just so she could run her fingers through his hair. It was smooth and silky, soft as a baby's. She'd touched his head before, but it had never felt like that. One of them had moved just a little then and their lips made contact. There was no urgency in what they did, but it was forceful.

Everything about Matt was angular with hard edges. His lips, however, were incredibly soft. The kiss itself was more than she could ever have expected: just the right amount of pressure, of wetness, of caressing. But it was what went through her mind that set it apart from others she'd had. Suddenly, they weren't Matt and Taryn sitting on a bench in the Opryland Hotel. They were on a boat, a gondola, and moving down the canals in Venice. And then she was in starched linens, a hoop skirt, and his skin was as black as coal. They changed over and over again until her head was dizzy.

When they pulled apart, it took her a moment to even remember where they were. He'd just been Matt then, thin with shaggy hair and an awkward build.

Nothing ever happened again. He took her home and didn't see her until New Year's Eve. They never talked about the kiss.

He'd had his chance, both before and after Andrew. He never took it. He couldn't be mad, now, that she was trying to move on.

The phone rang late, nearly midnight. She must have fallen asleep watching television because the sound was far away, like an echo. When she answered the call she felt disoriented and lost.

"Taryn?!" It was Daniel and he was frantic.

"Daniel, are you okay?" She rubbed at her eyes and sat up in bed. It was dark, the television screen cast an eerie glow about her room. She fumbled for the switch on her lamp and looked at the clock on the nightstand. "What's the matter?"

"The tavern's on fire!" he shouted. "It's in flames."

"What!" Jumping out of bed, she ran to her window as though she could actually see the tavern through the miles. "What happened?"

"We don't know. The fire chief is here. They put everything out. Well, mostly. You can still see flames. The worst of it is gone. It got the back part, half of the tavern. They think it might have been arson."

"Oh my God," Taryn cried. "Why would somebody do that?"

"Insurance money," Daniel replied bitterly. "People do shit like this all the time. They called me and I got here as fast as I could. Luckily, someone was driving down the highway and saw the smoke and flames and called the police. If they hadn't been quick the whole thing would've been gone."

"I am so sorry," she apologized. "That's horrible."

"Yeah, well, if it's someone trying to cause trouble they may be back. I think it's important from now on that you only come out here in the daytime. Not by yourself at night," he lectured.

"No worries. I don't do night trips anymore," she promised. "Take care and I'll talk to you tomorrow."

She hung up the phone feeling dazed. Who the hell would do something like that? The building had stood more than one-hundred fifty years and someone just randomly one day decided to destroy it, quite possibly for the fun of it? People were crazy.

A few minutes later her phone beeped. It was Matt.

"Found your descendent. Sent her an email and pretended to be you. Hear from her soon."

Chapter 16

*F*rom the front, at least, the tavern appeared intact.

Or, at least, as intact as it had looked since her arrival. She could smell an acrid, charred scent, though, and thin wisps of smoke were still curling into the sky. When she walked around to the back she could see half a dozen firemen trudging through the ruins and poking at piles of black lumber and bricks, putting out small flames with hoses. The entire tavern part was gone, leaving a gaping hole in the back, making it look like someone who'd been caught with their skirts up. It was overcast and calling for rain. What even a week of being exposed could do to that part of the house might just be irreversible.

"I know what you're thinking," Daniel sighed. "The back of the house there being open. Some friends got together with tarps and big tents and stuff. We're going to cover it up as soon as the firemen leave."

That would help, for now. "Do they have any idea who did this?"

Daniel shrugged. He looked rough and wild, like he'd been up all night. There were even smudges of black on his face as though, he, too had tried to jump into the rubble and pull something out. "They think maybe just kids. Only one who would stand to gain anything by setting it on fire is the owners and they're in New York this week, visiting family."

"Doesn't mean they couldn't have hired someone to do it," Taryn pointed out.

"Yeah, I know. Fact is, it doesn't matter. This will put us so far over our projected budget I don't think we'll ever get there now. We only have a week."

"What's your campaign up to?"

"That's the thing; it was actually doing pretty good. We were up to almost $8,000. My professor, the one who pulled out? He had a change of heart and went back in. Wouldn't tell me why. Brought in some other friends, too."

Taryn smiled and patted him on the arm. "Well, maybe this will turn into a blessing in disguise. People like to jump in and help during tragedies. You never know. It might bring in even more money."

"I know," Daniel tugged at his bears peppered with ash. "I thought about it. But damn it, why the tavern? That part hadn't even changed much since the 1800s."

When Taryn got back to the B&B she turned off the television, put a CD in her laptop (Caroline Herring's haunting "Lantana") and brought out a clean canvas. In her painting for Daniel and his organization she'd been working on a profile of the inn and the tavern, showing a little bit of everything. It wasn't a difficult project because as poor of shape as the building was in, it was still whole. She didn't have to use her talent for anything more than prettying it up, more or less.

Now, with the tavern gone, she focused on doing what she did best—seeing things that weren't there. This picture would be completely dedicated to the tavern end and nothing else. She had tons of photographs of it and her memory would serve her as well. The rest she would make up.

On the top part of the canvas she used charcoal to sketch the exterior of the tavern. It was one story, brick, with a line of windows running down the side. A small porch extended from the side entrance, just big enough for two or three people to stand on at once.

At the bottom she sketched the interior. Here, she drew tables, a bar, chairs, a wide enough place at the back that could be used for dancing. She didn't include any people, but left plates and bowls on the table, glasses on the bar, lanterns lit...it appeared as though everyone had simply got up and walked away one night. The two images she blended together with the front of the inn between them so both appeared to fade in and out of it.

It took her nearly two hours to do the rendering and she went through three charcoal sticks. By then, she was exhausted and hungry. She was almost finished with the main painting, but would work on this one in the evenings and then present it as a gift to Daniel before she left. If they were able to raise the money they might be able to use it. If not, she hoped he would at least appreciate it for sentimental value.

Chapter 17

Dear Taryn,

It was so nice to hear from you. I've recently gotten into genealogy, thanks to Ancestry.com, so your email came as a wonderful surprise to me. I know a little about my great-great grandfather Elijah from stories my grandpa told. I also knew of his sister, Permelia, but mostly from the letters she sent home. Although she never returned to Boston after moving to Indiana to be with her husband, she wrote home frequently. She corresponded regularly with her sister, my great-great-great Aunt Lucy, and her mother. As an only child and descendent I was lucky enough to acquire these when my mother passed away recently.

I've scanned the letters I have and attached them. There aren't too many but I hope they help. Please let me know if I can help you in any other way.

I'd love to see any pictures you've taken and look at your painting once it's finished. I've seen one image of the tavern in an old history book, but it wasn't very plain.

Sincerely,
Eve

Taryn closed her eyes, exhilaration rushing through her. Matt had come through for her; she was finally going to get somewhere. The fire was a slap in the face; seeing the damage was awful. But then, when he told her about the email, she'd been uplifted. Letters would definitely help, Taryn thought with excitement. If nothing else they would give her an insight to Permelia's personality and maybe a little more information as to what she might want.

Settling down into her pillow, Taryn started reading.

October 1, 1839

Dear Lucy,

We arrived by stagecoach yesterday and the ride was not as awful as I'd feared. The air was cold in the evening but I was wrapped snuggly and there were blankets and rugs to help take the chill off. I am sure you want to hear all about my marriage and not my transportation, however.

I met James three days ago. He was awaiting my arrival and was almost exactly the way he'd described himself. I say "almost" because I find him much more

245

attractive than what he had boasted. He is a tall man with black hair and blue eyes. He says his ancestors are from Ireland, although he has been here for three generations. He is lively of spirit and animated. He can tell raucous jokes with the other men and is yet still tender and gentle with me. He has made me laugh many times on the journey and for that I am grateful.

The tavern is much pleasanter than expected. We have a set of rooms that are spacious and well-equipped. My trunks take up much space but James doesn't mind. I know Father is not keen on my being a proprietor of such an establishment but, I can assure you, it is a well-respected title here and James is looked upon in favor.

We do have many people working here. We have several servants who help with the cooking, the cleaning, the maintenance. Lydia has been with James from the beginning. She is the cook and her husband, Paul, takes care of the horses. We've made close friends with one another and she's teaching me what I need to know.

Please write when you are able to.

Much love,
Permelia

September 22, 1840

Dear Lucy,

It is difficult to believe I have lived here for almost a year. The first few months were lonely and I was terribly homesick. I thought of you constantly and cried myself to sleep on many occasions. Being an adult is more difficult than I imagined. It's difficult enough to be a wife; looking after dozens of strangers every night and ensuring that each traveler is well taken care of and tended to is nigh on exhausting. Many times I've longed to be back in Boston with you, walking through the gardens or enjoying a recital. Simply laughing again with another woman would be ideal. I do feel, however, that I am becoming accustomed to this life and it is starting to bring me joy. I enjoy meeting the new travelers, hearing their stories, and tending to them. We haven't any children yet but I think of those weary souls as mine, in a sense.

I am sorry Father is still not speaking of me. I did write him a letter but he did not respond. Please tell him I send my love.

Permelia

February 5, 1841

Dearest Mother,

I do hope this letter finds you well and in good health. I think about you daily and wonder how you are doing. I have settled into my role here at Griffith Tavern and although there are days that are trying, I do love it here. I also love my husband. He is a strong, kind, and generous man. We are partners as much as we are husband and wife and this is deeply satisfying to me. Although we run our business and I play hostess to the guests each night, it is late when everyone has turned in and it's just the two of us when I am the happiest. We often stay up until dawn, simply enjoying one another's company and talking. His companionship means the world to me, just as yours did.

I know I didn't do a good job of explaining why I left Boston. The truth is, I have always had a yearning in me to see more and do more. When I looked at the other young women and the lives they were settling into, I saw their happiness but I also saw the sameness in what they were doing. I did not feel that was the life for me. This life I have chosen is difficult and trying, but it does make me happy.

The tavern is struggling a little. Our guests come at an influx or else there is a dry spell. Sometimes they barter for their rooms and meals. Although this occasionally does work to our advantage, like many people we also need the coins. When they are not able to pay, we suffer as well.

We hoped to have a child by now and, indeed, I was with child for a short time period. I caught an illness, however, and the doctor thought it traveled to the child I carried. He does think we will go on to have more children. That is my one true hope. I wish to fill our home with laughter and song from those who belong to us.

Please tell Father I send my best. I love you and think of you every day.

Yours,
Permelia

May 26, 1841

Dear Lucy,

I am sorry it has taken me so long to respond to your last letter. We have been ever so busy here at the tavern and inn. More and more people continue to come through and stop and I feel as though I am constantly moving around, tending to others. My back and feet ache at the end of every day but it's a happy kind of fatigue I feel. We are thriving in our purse and James is delighted at our progress. We hosted a party three nights ago and it continued until dawn. I love dancing so much, as you know, and although my feet were bleeding by the time I went upstairs to our rooms I don't think I've ever been as happy.

We did experience one mishap recently. A month ago, one of our boarders partook in the whiskey a little too strongly. He wandered away from the tavern in the early morning hours and fell into the large hole in the back. We try to warn our guests about these, and most abide, but we assume he must not have been in his right senses. He was not traveling with his family and seemed to be alone in the world. This may have been a blessing in disguise because at least there is no one to mourn him

I am so very happy to learn of your engagement. I would like to attend your wedding but am currently unable to travel since I am now carrying a child. Yes, it is happy news and a good time for both of us. I am certain you will look lovely in your dress and please know I will be thinking of you and all the happiness you deserve.

Love,

Permelia

September 9, 1841

Dear Mother,

As I grow nearer to my birthing I am reminded of the sacrifices you made for your children and I yearn to be closer to you. I have a few trusted women here to help me, but none of them are replacements for my mother. I am more than a little frightened, but I know I will come through the ordeal and, when I do, will be blessed with what James and I have so patiently waited for.

Several new inns have been built here in town but ours remains the most popular. Many guests say it is due to the food. I like to think I have something to do with that. I discovered my talent for baking and cooking upon moving here. Naturally, as I near the end of my condition, we have hired others to perform those duties so I may rest more.

We did recently build a pavilion. It's beautiful and just right off the tavern. It will be glorious next summer when we can have music there and guests can enjoy the warm evenings in it. We use it now on nights that aren't too chilly.

Please remember to say a prayer for me and my child when the time comes.

Love truly,
Permelia

November 8, 1841

Dear Lucy,

I have more respect now for our mother, and all mothers, than ever before. Birthing was an ordeal I'd wish to forget. I knew I was dying at one moment, although the women around me said all women think that. I did deliver a healthy baby girl, however, and that is the important thing. We named her Hannah Rachel. She is an absolute angel and rarely makes a peep. I am completely in love with her, as is James. She is the light of the tavern and all the guests wish to make her acquaintance on a nightly basis. Oh, how I wish you could see her! And I wish I could have been in attendance at your wedding. Mother said Father didn't

want me there at all. I am afraid he still feels shame about
my departure. I did so hope he was come around in time.

Do know I love you and think about you daily.

Yours,
Permelia

April 16, 1842

Dear Mother,

I hoped to write sooner, but was quite unable. I trust
you received the letter from James himself. He read me
aloud the words he wrote to you and I felt them adequate,
although no words can ever describe our true grief.

The preacher said our Hannah was too good for this
world, too pure. We had more than one hundred souls in
attendance for her small, sad funeral. The inn was shut
down for almost an entire week, although visitors still came
and brought food, drinks, and other items of comfort. One
young woman made me a beautiful quilt and another
brought me a wreath she made of dried flowers and berries.
We still have it hanging on our door. I am blessed beyond

compare to live in such a place where people are kind, attentive.

Hannah was not ill. She simply passed on as she slept. When I awoke the morning felt too late. I realized she had slept through her feeding and changing. The cold dread that ran through my veins was perhaps mother's intuition. I knew she was gone before I approached her bed. Still, I hoped.

Her little mouth was drawn in a smile, her cheeks still flushed as though she was merely sleeping. Her tiny hands curled around the blanket you sent her. But she was cold, oh so cold. I held her and wept until James pried her out of my arms and took her away. His grief is insurmountable. She was his angel. I mourn as well, but Lydia has proven to be a rock for me in this time. James, I fear, has no one. He will not speak to me about it.

The doctor says we will have more. I am not sure I will be able to carry another; the burden in my heart is too heavy.

Permelia

December 10, 1842

Dear Lucy,

Here is wishing you and your family a wonderful Merry Christmas. I hope it is filled with love and laughter. The inn is alive with wonderment. We invite the local children to meet St. Nicholas here. James is busy giving away sweets. He's even bought toys to hand out to everyone. It is a festive atmosphere and I am trying my very best to stay happy and merry for everyone.

Please pass on my love to Father.

Yours truly,
Permelia

October 21, 1846

Dear Lucy,

Another tragedy has struck us. Sometimes it feels as though grief and hurt will never leave. My beloved James was killed last week when his horse threw him to the ground. We buried him two days later. I am a widow now and do not quite know what to do with myself. James was more than just my husband, he was my friend. I was connected to him in ways I never thought imaginable. He was the light of this inn, a beautiful soul. I could not have asked for anyone to be better to me, or to love me more.

My bed is so cold now; cold and lonesome. I have sent word to Mother to inquire about coming home. I don't wish to stay here any longer. How can I without my love?

Permelia

December 1, 1846

Dear Lucy,

Thank you for your generous offer. I do not think any household is large enough for two families, however, and with your husband and dear children already in yours I fear I would only be in the way. It is unfortunate Father won't welcome me back into his home. I will find a way to survive here, never fear. It breaks my heart but I am strong and will find a way to become stronger. I have difficult decisions to make ahead, but I will make them, even if they break my heart.

Take care my dear,
Permelia

There were no more letters. They'd either been lost through the years or Permelia had simply stopped writing. When she was finished reading them she'd gone for a walk. Now she sat back in her rocking chair on the porch and gazed out into the yard. The reading had left her emotionally drained. Before, Permelia had simply been a character in history, a name. And a face. But now she was a real living and breathing person. She'd been someone who enjoyed her work, had loved her husband, had yearned for a child and then lost one. She hadn't gone back to her family in Boston because they didn't want her. She stayed here not out of love but because she had no other viable option. It had, perhaps, been desperation that made the tavern and inn so successful after her husband's death; failure simply wasn't an option for Permelia.

She'd been a fairly young woman when her husband was killed. And she'd lived to be almost ninety. All those years running the tavern alone...

Maybe this was what she wanted, Taryn thought. Maybe she just wanted to be known. LeRoy had mentioned a baby. Hannah had only lived a few months by Taryn's estimation. History hadn't deemed her important. She could find her grave, place flowers on it. Maybe that's what Permelia needed; she needed her story known and had chosen Taryn to tell it. Now, at least, the tavern might be demolished but Permelia and her family wouldn't be forgotten.

Maybe that was enough, Taryn closed her eyes and gently rocked; maybe it was enough.

Taryn called Miranda later that afternoon.

"Oh, honey, it's just awful what happened out there," Miranda fretted. "Just awful. I bet it was somebody on drugs."

Taryn didn't feel like pointing out that arsonists weren't normally addicts, but she hadn't made the phone call to show off her mad profiling skills. "It is terrible," she agreed instead. "The Friends of Griffith Tavern are disappointed."

"Well I'd say they are!" Miranda squealed. "I'm so glad it wasn't one of our beautiful historical homes here in town. At least that's something to be thankful for."

It angered Taryn that one of the "historical homes," which wasn't nearly as old as the tavern but was undoubtedly better maintained and pretty, was valued more. "I guess that's something anyway…" she replied philosophically.

"Have you had any luck tracking down any of the family members?"

Taryn briefly filled her in on Matt's success and Eve's correspondence, as well as the content of Permelia's letters. "I'll send you the email, too," she said. "It has all the letters attached to it."

"That poor thing," Miranda sighed. "Of course, we didn't know she'd lost a child."

"Where do you think her baby is buried?" Taryn asked. "I've walked around the property, but haven't seen any graves."

"More than likely in the city cemetery then," Miranda explained. "That's where Permelia and James are buried. My guess is her little grave is somewhere close by. There are many infants buried there. Some don't have names so we can't be sure who they are. Some don't have any markings at all and we can only guess they're children by the size of their headstones."

Taryn received directions for the cemetery and hung up. She'd find it then.

"If you're listening, P, I just wanted to let you know I'm going to go look for your baby's grave and decorate it. Hope that's okay."

The lamp on her nightstand flickered once, then again, and then all was still.

Taryn technically didn't *have* to drive to the cemetery, since it was only a few blocks away, but she did because the only place that sold flowers was on the other side of town. Their arrangements were all pricey but she was pretty handy when it came to making her own so she bought some Styrofoam, a spool of wire, wire cutters, and several loose flowers for half the price a pre-made arrangement cost. Taryn believed in being industrious and thrifty when the situation called for it.

Despite the town's small size, the cemetery was enormous. Two big wrought iron gates flanked the wide entrance with stone lions on either side. Their great mouths were open in a yawn, baring great teeth. The lions were turning green with age and one of the gates was almost off its hinges, dangling a little in the wind. The road inside was sparkling white gravel and wove through the rows in curves and circles. Permelia and James were buried at the front, near the entrance, so she didn't have far to go. With her bag of goodies in hand, she got out and began walking around, studying the headstones.

It was easy enough to find James and Permelia. They were in the second row with only one grave separating them from the end. Their headstone was modest in size, but boasted their names in large letters. Under their names were the words "Together in life, together in death." Like most of the graves in the cemetery, it was without flowers or any kind of adornment. The stone was weathered with age and chipped in a few places. The grass was getting tall, too, a little above her ankles. She assumed the city maintained it, but with trash blowing around and the overall shabbiness, it didn't look like it was high on their list of priorities.

The graves surrounding Permelia and James were dated in the mid to late 19th century and early 20th century. They varied in sizes and designs, but were definitely all adults. She slowly walked back and forth, taking care to read the dates and names, but couldn't see an infant's grave on the row in front or behind them. Soon, she came to a clump of graves with death dates all within the same year or two. They had to be from the war, Taryn figured, since the time period was right. The Civil War hadn't touched this place in terms of battle but of course men would've gone off to fight. There were at least a dozen headstones of young men, standing in a row together like the soldiers they were in real life.

Hannah had to be buried somewhere. Of course, it was possible she'd been buried on the tavern's property and the headstone had merely been moved or destroyed over the years. If that were true, she'd never find it.

Taryn was about to give up when she took one last look around, just in case she'd missed something. A weeping willow tree grew several rows behind Permelia and James and the long, dried-up branches brushed at the ground. It was under the tree, up against the trunk, that she found what she was looking for. It was only about a foot and a half tall and had a small stone lamb atop. The headstone read:

H.R.B.
Not dead, just sleeping

She wasn't prepared to feel the sharp pang, seeing this grave of a baby who would be dead by now even if she had survived her infancy. But a heaviness filled her chest and she could feel tingling in her nose, something she referred to as "the nose stage" which signified an impending onslaught of tears. She quickly sat down on the ground beside the little headstone and got out her materials. She'd chosen bright yellow daises and soft pink roses for the arrangements. The flowers themselves might not go together, but they were her two favorite and she wanted something happy and sunny for little Hannah.

While she worked, she talked to the grave.

"I didn't know you or your mama, of course, but I've gotten to know her a little. I can't tell you what happened when you went to sleep that night and didn't wake up but I can assure you that you were wanted and your parents loved you very much. I guess you knew that, though. You would've felt it."

The cemetery was quiet; the only sound was the crinkling of paper trash as it hit up against the side of the fence.

"I'm making you an arrangement because, well, I'm a little broke and also because I think it's more personal. Now, I know a professional would probably look at this and be appalled but I think it turned out pretty well."

She sat back and admired her handy work before placing the arrangement in the container and sticking it in the ground. At least now Hannah's grave looked a little cheerier.

Taryn got up, dusted off her pants, and walked back to Permelia's gravesite. She had three red live roses for her and these she placed atop the stone. "I want you to know your child has been acknowledged. The historical society knows about her, I know about her, and we won't forget.

Your letters will go on display and anyone who wants to read them will know more about your life. So maybe this will give you a little bit of peace."

Taking a deep breath, she continued. "And I know about what happened with the man. I am so sorry. If you lived today you'd see all kinds of pamphlets and articles and stuff telling you it wasn't your fault, that you didn't provoke it, and that there's help available for you. But I'm guessing you didn't get that so much back then. So I'll have to tell you that myself: It wasn't your fault, you didn't provoke it, and I am sorry. I am angry and hurt for you. But it's over now. It's time for you to move on."

A strong gust of wind flew around the headstone and Taryn's hair whipped back from her face, streaming out behind her, the curls bouncing against her back. One of the red roses gently lifted from the headstone and when Taryn reached over to stop it from blowing off, it merely laid itself back down to rest. The wind stopped.

Taking that as a cue, Taryn turned and left.

When she reached Matt around suppertime he was more subdued than usual. "I'm sorry," he finally said at last. "I guess I panicked."

"Why?"

"I don't know," he replied. "For almost all of my life you were mine, and then you were Andrew's. When Andrew died you and I were, you know... I didn't see you. And then I got you back and it felt like you were mine again. Knowing you're seeing other people makes me feel like I'm losing you again."

The idea made her sad and she didn't know how to begin making either one of them feel better. "Well, first of all, no matter what I do you can't lose me. Even if we go years without talking, which we have, you're still a part of me. And secondly, you know I don't *belong* to anyone. It doesn't matter if I'm married, single, dating, or join a convent."

"I know that," he mumbled. "And that hurts in a different way."

"For God's sake, how?" she demanded.

But he changed the subject.

"I'm sorry about the tavern. I would've texted back but I was in the middle of a meeting." Matt worked for NASA, her own rocket scientist, but they communicated so frequently it was hard for her to remember sometimes he had a job. He worked all hours of the day and night, sometimes even from home, and she had never truly been sure of what it was he actually *did.*

"Don't worry about me. Work. I want to be able to tell everyone one day that I know someone who has traveled to outer space."

"I'm not an astronaut, but I will go up at least once," he agreed.

"And I'll be there to wave you off. And see you come back."

"If I come back at night, don't bother," he advised. "I've seen a ship land at night and it's not nearly as interesting as you think it would be."

She laughed. Only Matt could find something boring about a spaceship landing.

Later in the conversation she told him about the letters, about her visit to the cemetery. Matt was quiet while he listened.

"Do you think that's it, then?" she asked when she was finished. "That maybe Permelia just wants her child and maybe herself to be known, acknowledged? That maybe it will stop now and she'll be at peace?"

"I don't know," he answered with hesitation. "It seems to me if that's all she wanted she would've asked for it a long time ago."

Taryn felt the same; she just didn't want to admit it.

"Maybe she didn't know how. I don't know what else to do. I also have something else to share…" She briefly told him about the dream she'd had a few nights before. It still shook her to think about it.

"You've always had bad nightmares," he pointed out. He knew she didn't like to sleep alone. When they were together she even slept with him, though in a purely platonic way.

"This felt different. I didn't know I was asleep."

"Do you think it's connected to what's going on?"

"Maybe," she answered. "Something didn't feel right. I didn't feel like myself. I could feel it, but I was also watching it."

"Can you send me the letters?" he asked. "I'd like to take a look at them myself. Maybe you're missing something and you just need an extra set of eyes."

Taryn agreed. There was something else playing at the back of her mind, but she couldn't put her finger on it.

Chapter 18

*M*att texted her twice the next day and called her

once but she didn't hear from Jamie at all. She didn't hear from Jamie the next day, either, although she sent him a text and tried to call. Her call went straight to his voicemail. She was disappointed he hadn't contacted her since the tavern caught on fire. He *had* to know about it; it was the biggest news in town. She'd seen more people come out to the property and wander around since the fire than she'd seen the whole time she'd been there. (And not just at the tavern, but period.) Now that it was threatened it felt like the townspeople were actually concerned about what might happen to it.

She'd been right about the reaction, too. Daniel's campaign was now up to a whopping $32,184. He was over his head with excitement, texting and emailing her every time a new donation came in.

She worked feverishly day and night, now, attempting to finish not one painting but two.

The B&B was quiet. A couple with young children stayed the weekend and seemed to wear Delphina out. She now moved with less energy, almost sluggish, her mind appearing to be somewhere else. When asked if everything was alright, she blamed the forthcoming bad weather that would undoubtedly show up in a few weeks. "This time of year just gets me down I guess," she explained, sadness creeping into her voice. "I can feel the cold in my bones more and more every year."

She *did* express outrage over the burning of the tavern, shaking her head wearily and asking what the world was coming to. "Teenagers, probably," she'd muttered. "I just think kids are more destructive than they used to be. We've always had troublemakers but these days it feels like there's just more of them and the things they do are twice as bad."

Taryn had only been to the tavern twice since she'd visited the cemetery, but so far things were quiet. Maybe everything she had done *was* enough.

Taryn was expecting the package from the attorney, but it was still a blow when it arrived in the mail. She read through the documents three times before sinking down to her knees on the floor, the loose pieces of paper fluttering around her.

Her Aunt Sarah had been much better off than she'd expected. She didn't leave Taryn a fortune, but in total, she was almost $100,000 richer than she was the day before. Sarah had apparently been collecting stocks and bonds for years. She'd cashed them out a few months before her death.

The pictures the attorney sent of the house showed it was in a sorry state. The beautiful stately historical home, once white and glistening, was dingy gray with peeling paint and a sagging porch. Weeds were choked in the yard, trees in desperate need of pruning. A window was boarded up, the glass missing. Sarah had been living there alone? More than one hundred years before a fire had ripped through the house and burnt a section so now it looked asymmetrical.

Taryn didn't mind that, but in its neglect it made this stand out even more.

The house was Taryn's now.

Closing her eyes, she remembered being a child there, running up the mountain behind the house and losing herself in the dark, deep woods; always mindful of bears. Black bears lived around Sarah's house. You could see them sauntering across the dirt road that wound around the property. They were slow and lumbered, almost comical, but Sarah taught her not to underestimate them. "They're quicker than they look," she'd warned young Taryn.

She remembered slipping on one of Sarah's antique flannel nightgowns; she must have been about seven. It dragged to the floor and she had to lift the front with her fingertips when she walked. She had a guest room to sleep in but Sarah always welcomed her into her bed and, together, the two of them would snuggle down under the covers and watch movies or read books while a wood fire roared a few feet away. Sarah always had a fire going. Said it made her feel peaceful.

And then there was the Sarah who was always gardening, sitting outside in the dirt, her light-colored slacks stained from grass and mud. That silly floppy hat perched on her head and a dollop of sunscreen on her nose. She didn't mind most of her body getting burned but she didn't like a red nose. "Makes me look like Rudolph," she'd giggled. "Or a wino."

"What's a wino, Aunt Sarah?"

"Um, never mind. Don't tell your mother."

She was gone and that big, beautiful, mysterious house was all Taryn's. The house with its wide front porch, attic big enough to hold a dance in, old-fashioned kitchen with its pump and farmhouse sink. The house with its drafty bedrooms, winding staircase, little balcony on the front, and water that was always either too hot or too cold. The house with so many smells Taryn could never distinguish all of them—some sweet with perfume, others pungent like the earth and trees around it, and some smoky and mysterious. "This house holds time," Sarah had told her one night. "It clings to everything and remembers it."

But Sarah was gone now. And Taryn was alone.

By Wednesday the secondary painting was finished. She'd spent all afternoon working on it and now it stood in a corner of her room on its own easel, proudly staring at her bed. She stretched out and looked at it, studied it. The room may have been empty, but there was life and movement present. It felt like everyone had just stepped outside for a moment and would be right back. A feeling of anticipation hung in the air, expectancy. She didn't remember trying to paint that. The tavern was dark and dusky, shadowed. Yet the lanterns and lamps filled parts of it with a warm, welcoming glow. If you stared at it long enough you felt like you might be able to walk right into it, through the doors and to the bar.

She was pleased.

Her telephone clanged, causing her to jump. It was Matt.

"I think I may have something," he panted, excited.

"It's almost midnight. What's up?"

"I just got in from work but on the drive home I kept thinking about the letters. Two things jumped out at me and I couldn't put my finger on them. Then it came to me!"

"What? You'd better talk real fast."

"I'm trying! Okay. So in one letter she's talking about the inn struggling, right?"

"Yeah," Taryn nodded, even though he obviously couldn't see her.

"And then she's talking about building a pavilion. Doesn't that seem odd?"

"Yeah, but that was at least two months later. Maybe business picked up," she shrugged. "It could happen, especially in those days. Feast or famine and all."

"But what happened *between* those two letters," he asked with glee.

"I can't remember. What?"

"The man, the drunk man? The one who died by falling into the 'big hole', which I am assuming was some kind of sinkhole."

She could almost read his mind and it lit her up. "You think maybe Permelia or James killed him and made it look like an accident? And then took his money?"

"Sure, why not?"

"It could've happened," she conceded. "Although they seemed like nice people."

"Well, maybe they were. Maybe it was an accident. Or," he said slowly, "maybe he deserved it."

"How? How could you deserve to be murdered and have your body thrown in a sinkhole?"

"Your dreams."

She might have been a little slow but she caught what he was saying loud and clear. "You think maybe he's the same man who attacked Permelia and then either she or James killed him and disposed of the body?"

"Yes. And took his money."

"Geeze, that's cold. But, I'm sorry, good for them," she smirked, remembering the fear and pain she'd felt. The tearing.

"Not saying there wasn't some justification there," he agreed. "But that *may* be your mystery."

"It wasn't long after that she got pregnant and miscarried. And then, a year later, her baby died. I wonder if she felt guilty, if she felt like she was doing penance for what they did to the man."

"Life doesn't work like that, Taryn," Matt chided. "Whatever higher power there is wouldn't take something out on an innocent child. I don't believe in the whole 'sins of our father' thing."

"It wouldn't matter if that's the way life really worked or not," she pointed out. "What would matter is how Permelia felt about it. That doesn't have to be based on logic."

"She felt responsible over his death and felt guilty, especially after she lost her child, is that what you're saying? And that's maybe why the letters stopped?"

"Yes," Taryn whispered. "She couldn't face anyone from her past anymore. Her dad's anger and shame at her for marrying the way she did, her own guilt at what happened...She was punishing herself."

"But nobody would've blamed her," he said. "Not her. Things happened *to* her. She didn't make them happen."

They were both quiet, understanding they were no longer talking about Permelia.

Taryn paced around her room like a caged animal. She felt in her bones that Matt was right. Her dream was Permelia's reality. She'd wanted Taryn to know what happened to her, to feel her fear and terror. And, somehow, the man had died. Either Permelia or James had killed him or he really did accidentally fall into the sinkhole. But the subsequent money rush couldn't be a coincidence. Maybe they'd robbed his pockets or robbed his room after finding him dead. Or maybe she'd killed him in self-defense yet still feared for her own safety. They could hang a woman back then, and did.

It didn't matter. They were all dead now. And somehow Permelia and James had come up with the money to build their pavilion and stay afloat for a long time.

The television was set to a local channel so she could watch "Dancing with the Stars." She hadn't been paying much attention to it, but did now as something caught her ear. The 11 o'clock news was on and a name made her stop and turn around. Jamie's golden face appeared on her screen, a photograph of him flashing his wide smile. She stopped what she was doing and sat down on the edge of her bed.

"...when he didn't show up for work on Wednesday," the newscaster was announcing. "His truck is still in his driveway but the thirty-five-year-old man hasn't been spotted since Tuesday morning. Friends and family are asking for anyone with information to contact the Wise County sheriff's department at-"

Taryn was speechless, the blood drained from her face. Jamie had...disappeared? What the hell? No wonder he wasn't answering her calls and texts. What could've happened?

Unable to look at his face on the screen, she flipped off the television and moved to her window. It was pitch black outside, the nearest twinkling lights of Main Street muted in the fog. He only lived a mile from the B&B. And yet, he'd been that close and something awful had happened to him and she didn't even know it.

Unless...

She quickly shook the thought out of her head. She couldn't believe Jamie had anything to do with the fire. It was just a coincidence his disappearance had happened a day after the fire. He loved old buildings, loved to explore. He wouldn't destroy something like that. He wouldn't set it on fire and just leave.

Unless, of course, someone offered him money to do just that. Money could be a dangling carrot even the strongest had trouble resisting.

She struggled to get up the next morning. Getting dressed, brushing her hair, washing her face…all these things took energy she didn't have. She broke out into a sweat while brushing her teeth; this act alone was almost too much. When she went downstairs, Delphina took one look at her and came running over. "My Lord, child, are you sick?"

Taryn let her fuss over her, let her pour her some orange juice and brush the hair back from her forehead. "You don't feel hot," she murmured, "but you're white as a ghost and clammy."

"I don't think I slept well last night," Taryn explained weakly. She was hungry but after two bites of biscuit her stomach was cramping; bile rose in her throat.

"Well, no offense dear, but you look like you haven't slept in a week."

"I haven't been sleeping well," she admitted to this grandmotherly woman. It felt nice to be fawned over.

"Is it the room? Is it too hot, too cold? Do you need an extra pillow?"

"I think it's fine," she replied. "It's just me. I never sleep well anyway and in the past few months I've just felt rundown, you know?"

"You need to get yourself to a doctor," Delphina lectured. "I don't want to be an alarmist but that cancer can sneak up on you if you're not careful. I belong to the Women's Club here in town and we lose a member almost every year; women who looked and acted perfectly fine and then went to their doctor one day and found out they were eat up."

Well, that was a cheery thought first thing in the morning.

"I don't know if I'm truly sick. I've had a lot of...things...happen in the past few months. I guess I'm still trying to deal with them. And then last night I heard about Jamie's disappearance."

Delphina shook her head and took a seat across from Taryn, evidently reassured she wasn't going to drop over dead within the next few minutes. "Such an awful thing. And his mama is out of her mind. I don't have any children, of course, but I can only imagine what his poor parents much be going through. And I hadn't even thought about how you would feel. I'm very sorry."

She looked like she meant it and the compassion in her watery old eyes made Taryn feel like crying. She was used to people paying attention to her, most often in a professional capacity, but it was rare for someone to actually express concern. "I just hope he's okay."

"I hope so, too. You realize, Taryn, this isn't your fault," Delphina said gently.

Her kindness hurt. "I know," she whispered, tears burning her eyes.

"And your husband's death, it wasn't your fault either."

"We'd argued. I wasn't even that sick. Just tired. I could've gone with him."

"And died too? Would that have been better?" Delphina asked mildly.

"I don't know. For me, maybe. I don't know what kind of afterlife there really is, but it has to be better than what I feel here most of the time." She was never this honest with a virtual stranger, but she was exhausted and sometimes talking helped. She wasn't receiving any judgment for her words; she could sense that.

"Maybe it would've been better for you," Delphina agreed. "But for your friend, your Matt? What about him?

And others who care about you that you might not even realize. What about those you've worked for since? You've brought a different kind of joy to them."

"They would've found someone else," Taryn said curtly.

"Ah, yes, they would have," Delphina granted. "But that someone else wouldn't have been you. You must start valuing yourself and what you have to offer. Nobody else can take your place."

Taryn smiled at the words and sentiment. "I don't always feel this way. I guess I'm just a little down."

"I don't blame you. I understand. When my own husband left I also considered leaving this world, if you understand my meaning. He was my life, my friend. I felt like I had nothing but him. I still feel that way sometimes, despite the fact I fill my days with the Women's Club, the Gardening Club, and all those other silly things taking up time and energy. Sometimes I feel like my life has been in limbo since he left, like I'm just waiting for the next part to start."

"I feel that way, too," Taryn said. "I thought Jamie was helping that."

Pain clouded Delphina's eyes and she reached across the table and took Taryn's hand in her own. "The important thing is that you took the step. Next time, it will be even easier. Your strength is within *you*, not gathered from someone else. You must remember that."

Taryn put the finishing strokes on her main painting that night. She'd let it rest for a day and then go back to it with fresh eyes and make any necessary changes. Daniel had written her earlier; their bank loan was denied. He was up to almost $70,000 in donations but that was barely half of what they needed. Their option ended at the end of the week. They wouldn't be able to buy it.

"The damn developer was out here today, walking around with his little crew and making notes," he complained. "The owners were here, too. They didn't look happy but they almost looked, *relieved* I guess. Their financial troubles will be over when they get paid. And the tavern will be gone."

"Daniel, let me ask you something..." She was curled up in the white wicker chair by her window, watching the front yard where Delphina was strolling around her rose bushes, lovingly clipping them back.

"Yeah, shoot."

"You just graduated from college. And the other members in your group, they're still there. What happens to the Friends of Griffith Tavern when you've all graduated and gone your separate ways? I had a professor once who said college was a horrible place to meet someone you wanted to marry because everyone was just in transition."

Daniel sighed. "I'm not going anywhere. This is my home. I actually have a good job with the state. I commute. And the others, well, I know they'll scatter. This holds their interest as long as they're here, but I can't expect them to be as passionate about it as I am. That's why I'm constantly recruiting new, younger members. We might have a big turnover, but as long as the passion is there that's what matters."

"And if the tavern becomes demolished? What then? What happens to your organization?"

"It's gone. But maybe I'll form another one, a more general one for historical preservation. There's always something needing to be saved," he declared.

Taryn hung up the phone feeling depressed. They'd tried but almost certainly failed. It would be gone and everyone would move on, including her. Permelia's dream was over. James' vision was gone. Time had moved on and left them behind a long time ago, just like time had moved on and left her and Andrew in the past.

Feeling like her world was not so much crumbling but slowly dissolving into oblivion, Taryn walked over to her bed and fell down to it. She cried silently at first, and then loudly. Huge wracking sobs that physically hurt her. She cried until her nose and throat were raw. She cried for Andrew, for his boyish good looks that would never grow old or never fade. She cried for his enthusiasm, his warmth, his ability to make everyone in the room feel special. She cried for his passion for historical architecture, his love of the past and the fact that he was now a part of it. She cried because it wasn't fair that she could see other people's ghosts but he had never once visited her; he'd moved on as surely she could not.

Then she cried for herself. She cried out of pity for her inability to look at anything she did without thinking how much better it would be if Andrew were with her. She cried for her lack of close girlfriends, for her lack of family. She cried for her head that seemed to hurt all the time, for the sleep she wasn't able to get, for her body she constantly fought with. She cried for her parents who loved her but didn't know how to show it, for her grandmother who had showed it but then left her alone too soon, for Jamie she was just getting to know and like.

Lastly, she cried for Matt. She cried because she wanted to feel him next to her, his arms around her. She wanted to feel his forehead pressing into hers again, wanted to feel that silky smoothness of his hair under her fingers again. She cried because she was afraid she'd kept him on the back burner too long and that the chance with him was gone, swept away by her selfishness.

When she was finished crying she got up, blew her nose, turned her pillow over to the dry side, and turned on her television. Some channel was playing the original "The Amityville Horror." She left it on.

Then, she went to her phone. Pulling up Matt's name, she typed:

Travis Tritt's "Anymore"

And closed her eyes as she sent "send."

Chapter 19

"It's absolutely amazing," Daniel breathed. The

painting was propped up against the wall, resting on the table in the café's booth. Joe and the others gathered around it and all made the appropriate "oohs" and "ahhs."

"I mean, I knew you could paint well, but this is truly unbelievable. I feel like I could walk right into it. You can see the lines in the brick, the roughness of the wood," Joe said enthusiastically. "It's hard to believe this is even a painting."

"Believe it or not, I get flack for that," Taryn laughed. "People say I shouldn't paint to look like photographs. That I should just photograph if I want it to be so realistic."

"Yeah, well, I don't know anything about art but this looks like it to me. And it's exactly what we needed," Daniel said sincerely.

"I'm glad you like it because..." Taryn let her voice trail off as she reached down into her cotton carrying case and pulled out the second painting, "I also did this. No extra charge, just a present."

The group was silent as they gathered in closer. She watched Daniel's eyes as they first lit up and then dampened. "It's beautiful. Even better than the other one. I can't believe you were able to do this."

"After the fire I thought you might want something to remember the tavern by. And so your architect will have something better to work with," she added.

Everyone was silent as they gazed down at their hands and feet. Finally, Joe spoke. "There isn't going to be any renovation. We lose our option to purchase in a few days. We don't have the money. It's over."

The others nodded.

"It's not over until it's over," Taryn avowed. "Something could *still* happen."

"Yeah," Willow smirked. "Something *bad*. They're talking about a Jamison's and a Target. Not that I don't want more shopping options here, but I don't know that I can stick around and watch. I love that old place. And what happened there...it makes me feel a part of it."

"We all read Permelia's letters," Daniel explained, wrapping an arm around Willow's waist. "We all feel a little closer to her now."

"Her baby died, her husband died, and she was STILL able to run it, carry on business as usual," Willow exclaimed. "How can you not admire someone like that?"

Taryn hadn't told Daniel what she and Matt had come up with in regards to the drunken traveler and his untimely drop into the sinkhole. Maybe nobody needed to know that. Maybe it didn't make a difference.

"I'm sorry to have to go," Taryn said. "I feel like I'm leaving you in a lurch." Her plane left the day after tomorrow. And then it was back to Nashville for a few weeks until she sorted out her next job. At least all the bills were paid.

"We'll keep in touch, though," Daniel said. "Hopefully we'll need you for another project in the future."

Matt hadn't written her back yet. That stung. Normally he'd respond at least within the hour, if not

288

immediately. But he was busy and she had to remember that he wasn't at her beck and call, no matter how much she felt like she needed him. She needed to quit relying on him so much. He didn't belong to her.

For the first time ever she felt like she was leaving with something unfinished. Everything, other than her painting that is, was still hanging in the air, incomplete.

There was nothing she could do, though. She'd uncovered Permelia's attack and her unknown infant. What else was there to do? She'd done the job she was hired for. The tavern, Permelia, and Daniel couldn't expect any more out of her. She wasn't sure she had anything left to give.

The television didn't offer any further news about Jamie's disappearance. Neighbors last spotted him Sunday morning as he got in his truck and sped away. Later that night he'd come home. His truck was still in the driveway. Nobody saw him drive home, or knew where he'd been all day, but the investigators placed his disappearance to be sometime late Sunday night or very early Monday morning since he didn't report to the stables for work the next day. Nothing in the house was disturbed but they were not ruling out a robbery. Taryn had a dozen questions to ask: was there still money in his bank account, did he seem upset Sunday morning, did he use his credit card on Sunday, was he in any kind of financial trouble, had any large deposits been made to his account, etc. But she figured the detectives were probably on top of that and didn't need her help.

Someone had come by and talked to her, a Detective Sallee. She didn't have much to add, she was sorry to say. She wished she did. As one of the last people to see him, though, they'd had to ask.

Taryn busied herself with packing her bags. It always took her at least a day to pack since she was notorious for bringing everything but the kitchen sink. She knew how to pack lightly; she just preferred not to.

Leaving out only two changes of clothes and a few toiletries, she set her bags by her bedroom door. The fees for checked luggage had become so ridiculously high it had cut down on the number of suitcases she packed when she flew. It didn't cut down on how much stuff she brought, though. She'd just learned how to pack better and really stuff it in there.

She did need to talk to Delphina. She wanted to ask her if she could take her breakfast on the road since she'd need to get up early and wasn't much of a morning person to begin with. She hadn't seen Delphina much over the past few days, just here and there. Delphina had been even quitter than usual. Taryn wondered if Delphina would miss her when she was gone. Having basically lived with her for the past month, she thought she might miss the older woman.

They hadn't spent a lot of time together, but it was comforting to know she was there.

Delphina wasn't out in her gardens, on the porch, or in the kitchen. Her bedroom door was standing wide open, the bed made with military precision. Taryn wandered around, calling out her name, but nobody answered. She had to be there, though, because her car was in the driveway and Delphina never walked anywhere. It was too hard on her hips and knees, thanks to her arthritis.

She was about to give up and head back up the stairs when she noticed the basement door, usually chained and locked, was cracked open just a little. A thin ray of light shot out from around it. Opening it a little wider, Taryn poked her head inside and called down, "Delphina! Are you down there?"

There was no answer. The stairs were steep, and though illuminated by a naked light bulb dangling from the ceiling above them, they were still dark. She worried Delphina might have lost her balance and fallen. She didn't like nosing around, at least not in a house that was actually lived in, but what if she was down below, unconscious? Making an executive decision, and hoping she wasn't prying, she hurried down the stairs, making sure to hold onto the rickety bannister as she went. "Delphina?" she called again. Silence.

The main room at the bottom of the stairs was large and strangely empty. It had to be the cleanest basement she'd ever seen. There was a peculiar scent in the air, something strong and powerful, and Taryn couldn't put her finger on it. It made her eyes water a little and the further into the room she got, the more pungent the odor became. Still, it was clear Delphina wasn't in this room.

Noticing two closed doors off the main room, Taryn walked over to the first and opened it. This room was packed with gardening supplies: top soil, gloves that still had price tags dangling from them, spades, pruners, and rakes. Everything was neatly stacked on a large wooden table up against the wall or hanging from pegs. The floor looked neatly swept and recently cleaned. When she saw the carton of bleach on the table she realized that's what she was smelling, what was making her eyes burn. "Dang, she even bleaches her basement floor," she muttered aloud. "I had no idea she was such a germaphobe."

She quietly shut the door behind her and moved to the next. It took a few tugs to yank it open and when she did she was met with almost total darkness. This room lacked a window so she had to wait for her eyes to get adjusted. When they did, they settled on the large wooden table pushed into the corner.

"Jesus Christ!" Taryn screamed. Her breath caught in her throat, her heart thudded against her chest, and she grabbed onto the door handle to steady herself, sure she'd faint dead away. As she lurched, footsteps resonated behind her and a frail, old voice cried, "Oh dear."

For what seemed like an eternity, Delphina and Taryn stood looking at each other, neither making a move. Delphina held a large shovel in her hand. It was raised high above her but the arm holding it was trembling. Still, if she brought it down hard enough it could do some real damage and Taryn wasn't taking any chances. She wanted to rush back upstairs and forget the two bodies stuffed under the table in the little dark room, but there was no going back from that.

"Delphina," she uttered with dismay. "What happened? What have you *done*?"

Jamie's light blond hair was well-lit now that the soft light from the main room had trickled in and settled on his head. His face was pale and his body was scrunched up at an awkward angle but she made no mistake– it was him. His eyes were closed, thankfully, and except for a band of dried blood streaking his face he looked like he could've been sleeping.

The other body was little more than a rumble of clothes. Only a skeletal hand reached out and grazed the floor. She couldn't see a face. She was thankful for small favors.

Delphina raised the shovel a little higher and Taryn sized up her opportunity. She could definitely outrun her, but she might still get in a good swipe as she passed her on the way to the stairs. Taking her chances, she leapt into action and sprung past the old woman, moving with speed she hadn't felt in years. The shovel clamored to the floor with a loud "bang" and when Taryn reached the bottom stair she turned around and looked behind her. Delphina was crumpled on the floor, her head in her hands.

"Well, shit," Taryn muttered. She stopped moving and stared at her hostess. "Did you kill him? What have you done?" She was in shock now, feeling nothing but fear. But the sight of his face was still etched in her mind and she could feel the tears streaming down her face.

"I didn't mean to," Delphina sobbed, her voice muffled by her hands. "I'm so sorry, I'm so sorry, I'm so sorry." She rocked back and forth, her gray hair a blur in the shadowy light.

"What did you *do*?" Taryn wasn't about to go any closer, even now that Delphina was defenseless on the floor, but her desire to sprint was gone, too. She felt defeated. Oh, Jamie. And he'd been so beautiful, so *nice*.

"He was looking for me, just like you were. And I wouldn't have hit *you*, I swear! I thought you were a burglar!"

"Did you kill him on accident?" Taryn asked. "Then why didn't you call the cops?"

"Not an accident," Delphina whispered meekly. "I'd left the door open. I heard him on the stairs. I knew he'd find it. He was looking for me, or for you. Maybe he thought one of us was in trouble. I came up behind him and panicked. I pushed him. His head, oh his head, it hit the bottom stair and then his neck..."

Taryn could see it now. He'd lost his balance, faltered, and broken his neck on the way down—what she thought might have happened to Delphina. "But why didn't you just call out for him? Bring him back up?" She was crying openly now, little sobs escaping with each word.

"I know, I know," Delphina replied, her voice frail. "I should have done that. I wasn't thinking. I was just thinking about what he would find, how people would *know*..."

"That's your husband, isn't it?" Taryn asked as it dawned on her. "Did you kill him too? You killed him and kept his body down here!"

"No!" Delphina shouted, adamant. "*No*, I would never do that. I loved him. He...he died of a heart attack. He'd had a bad heart for years. I just dragged him down here. I kept up a vigil, though. I brought him flowers, took care of his body. I visit him almost every day."

"But that's..." Insane, she thought to herself. Crazy. "If it was a heart attack, why not just call an ambulance? Isn't that the logical thing to do?"

Delphina nodded, biting her lip. "It would've been, if there wasn't a complication. The thing is, we were never married. Nobody around here knows that. There were reasons in the beginning why we couldn't and then, as the years went by, we didn't see a reason to. It was just a piece of paper we told ourselves. Only, we hadn't thought far enough in the future. His pension, his social security. We depended on that. The B&B wasn't doing well enough for us to live on. Without his money, we wouldn't have made it."

Taryn could see it all now. "And if he was dead, you would stop drawing that. The money would be gone?"

"And what would I do then? He was my life. I only knew him and this house. I couldn't support myself, not on my social security alone. I know so many old women who end up in state nursing homes, barely living. Just surviving. I wasn't ready to give up yet."

"So you let people believe he left you, ran out, so that you could continue to draw his checks?" Taryn asked softly.

Delphina nodded miserably. "It was a terrible thing to do, but I didn't know what else. We have no children, no family. I would've lost my house, my livelihood. I might look like an old woman but I still feel forty most of the time. I didn't want my life to be over so soon. He would've understood," she said, looking in the direction of the room where his body lay. "He would have. He wanted to take care of me and this way he was, even in death."

"You have to report this, Delphina," Taryn said gently. "Jamie's parents don't know what happened to him. They deserve to know their son is dead and not out there, somewhere, hurt or afraid or being held prisoner by some psycho." She winced at her choice of words but went on. "And your husband...he deserves a proper burial. You know he does. This isn't fair for him or for you."

Delphina rose to her feet and gently shut the door to the small room that contained the bodies. "I know. The guilt has eaten me alive, like a cancer. I can't do it any longer. Will you help me?"

Taryn walked to her and put her arm around her thin shoulders. "We'll call the police together."

Hours later the police were still swarming the house, taking pictures and turning things upside down. It made Taryn sad to see the immaculate house in disorder. She knew it was the last thing she should be thinking about but Delphina always tried so hard to keep it neat and organized.

Taryn was interviewed twice, once at the house and once at the station. Since Delphina had admitted to everything, though, there was no real investigation. Still, because the house was a crime scene now she'd had to move her belongings to the nearest motel, a motor inn. Her bed actually vibrated for fifty cents.

She was still in shock. She would never get over the sight of Jamie's dead body or Delphina's husband's outstretched hand. She could still feel Jamie's kiss on her cheek, see the way he'd smiled at her...

But maybe even more, she'd never forget the look of sorrow and dismay as the police gently led Delphina from the house and helped her into the cruiser. She had killed, but she wasn't a murderer. In some ways, Taryn couldn't fault what she'd done with her husband. There was no excuse for what she'd done to Jamie, but her husband was a different matter.

You heard horror stories about those nursing homes. Where else would she have gone? Maybe government assisted apartments? The ones based on income? She guessed that was a choice. But the thought of giving up her beautiful home, her job, most of her furniture to live in a small one bedroom apartment, alone? She could see how that idea wasn't an enticing one.

Daniel was shocked. He'd offered to come over and bring Willow but Taryn declined. She wasn't in the mood to socialize. She felt somewhat responsible for Jamie's death. If she hadn't gone out with him, he wouldn't have been over there. Two deaths of two men she'd cared about and she'd been at the center of both.

Taryn alternated between crying and staring numbly into space. Maybe they'd been wrong. They'd thought Permelia was attracted to her because of the whole "single woman on her own" bit. But maybe that wasn't it at all. Maybe Permelia'd been attracted to her because she was responsible for Andrew's death, and now Jamie's, the same way Permelia was for the drunk guy who attacked her.

Maybe she saw a murderer in her.

But that couldn't be right. She hadn't killed Andrew; she was just feeling sorry for herself. And Jamie, poor Jamie, with his love of old houses and gentle way with horses. He was gone and would never ride again, never explore anything, never listen quietly with those big eyes...she hadn't even gotten to know him well and his life was just starting.

She knew grief would come later, maybe not even for months. But that didn't stop little moans and whimpers from escaping now.

Taryn sat on the slick generic bedspread and punched in another message to Matt. He still hadn't called her back or answered her texts. She was emotionally drained and needed him. It was starting to rain outside and the wind was picking up. A storm was coming.

She was sorry for Delphina, sorry for herself. She'd left her bags in the car and only brought in a change of clothes. The grimy motel bathtub didn't exactly scream bubble bath, or even shower, and there was nothing on television. She felt lost, abandoned.

What people did to survive...

Well, she'd survived on Andrew's insurance money after his accident. If it hadn't been for that she would've been out on her ass, the house probably foreclosed on. She'd depended on both their incomes to sustain the life she knew. With him gone, she'd had to learn a new way. Delphina had found a way to carry on as well, albeit a morbid one. And Permelia. She, too, had found a way to endure.

Taryn laid back on her bed and listened to the thunder rumbling. She hoped the tarp on the inn would hold out the rain water. Not that it would matter since it was probably going to get torn down anyway.

Taryn let the images of the day play through her mind again, a kind of movie reel of the horrible events. She could see the door opening into the dark room, Jamie's hair glistening in the light, Delphina standing before her with the shovel raised above her head. The police cars, their lights. Delphina staring out the cruiser window, a grief-stricken look on her face as she watched her house fade out of sight.

It was one for the books.

Then her mind fell to Permelia. That story was harder to visualize but, with the help of the letters, she could try. She saw her attacked, saw the attacker falling to the ground when her husband came in and caught him, dragging the body to the sinkhole after everyone was asleep and in bed, going through his room and searching for the money he kept...Then she saw her pregnant, giving birth, carrying around an infant dressed all in white while the guests cooed over her, waking up and finding her lifeless in her bed, getting the news her husband had fallen to his death, rejected by her family...

Taryn sat up with a start, blood draining from her face.

"Oh my god," she cried, slapping herself on the forehead. "How did we not see that before?"

The rain was coming down in torrents now so she slipped on a college hoodie and grabbed her flashlight and rain jacket. She should wait until morning but she might miss her flight if she did. Not making the same mistake she made last time, she picked up her phone and first called Daniel, telling him what was going on, and then left a message for Matt. Daniel and Willow promised to meet her at the house.

"If I'm right," she told him, "then this could be a VERY good thing."

"Let's hope so," he declared. "Let's hope so."

It took her more than half an hour to get to the tavern since the motel was in the next town over. She was sure Daniel would beat her but when she pulled up the property was vacant. She could barely see the inn through the rain. It was almost pitch black outside. Trying to curb her excitement and nervousness, she turned on some music and sang along, hoping the up-tempo song would help the time go by faster.

By the time the first song was over, though, and there was still no sign of Willow and Daniel she decided to take matters into her own hands. It wasn't like anyone was going to try to kill her this time. The only thing she had to fear was the dark. And the rain. And maybe a ghost. But the ghost *wanted* her help; she wouldn't hurt Taryn.

Shrieking from the wind and rain she ran to the porch, hunching over as though being closer to the ground would help her dodge the drops. It was different being there at night. Her mother told her that houses are different in the dark and that if you want to live in one you should always look at it in the afternoon and around midnight before you made your decision.

Giving the door a little shove, she stepped inside and turned on her flashlight. Despite her rain jacket, she was soaked through to the skin and cold. Miss Dixie was shoved down inside her hoodie and she pulled her out and got her ready. "We have some work to do, old girl," she declared. She could barely hear herself speak; the rain was deafening.

There wasn't any use heading towards the tavern (since it was no longer there) or even the sitting room. She knew where she needed to be.

Taking the stairs two at a time she loped up to the second story and entered the first bedroom, the small room where she'd seen the bloody handprint. "Do your thing," she advised as she turned on the camera, held her breath, and took a shot. The room instantly flashed with light and then

303

darkened again. For a second, though, before the light dimmed Taryn was sure she saw the outline of a bed, a dresser, and a nightstand.

She took a few more steps into the room and this time turned and faced the door. "And one more," she pronounced and pushed the button. The flash was like lightning as it streaked across the room. The burst of it and sudden disappearance made the room feel even darker and Taryn shivered. She'd put her flashlight in her rain jacket pocket and now she took it out again as she walked to Permelia's bedroom.

Standing in the middle of the room she closed her eyes and allowed the energy of the past to soak into her. "I'm here to help, here to help," she chanted. She tried to see Permelia, tried to feel the furnishings of the past around her, tried to hear the noises of the tavern below her. The lightning struck again and the roll of thunder that followed was so loud it shook the house. Her feet rocked under her and she parted them to gain her balance. The storm was right on top of her.

In this room, she took half a dozen pictures. Between her flash and the lightning the room lit up with a dizzying pace until she felt like she was on a dance floor with strobe lights. With each new burst Taryn felt more out of touch with herself, less grounded. She was in a dream again, a part of the darkness, a part of the room. "Show me what you want!"

she shouted above the earsplitting thunder and rain. "You have to help me help you!" Another shot and a glance down at her LCD screen had her screaming and jumping backwards. Permelia was standing mere feet from her; her sad, beautiful face streaked with tears (or rain) and her nightgown bloody and torn. Her outstretched hands were covered in mud and reaching for Taryn.

"Oh God," Taryn moaned. She fumbled with the button and took another shot; this time Permelia was even closer, almost close enough to touch Taryn's hair. Her fingernails were ripped and torn, a profound bruise on her cheek. When Taryn looked up from the camera into the dark room, it was empty. "I can't do this. I was wrong! I've got to get out of here."

Without turning on her flashlight she raced for the stairs. In the distance she saw a flash of light through the window. Daniel and Willow were here. She thought she could do this alone but she was wrong. She needed help.

"I'm inside," she hollered, though she knew it was useless. They'd never hear her. "In here!" If she could just make it to the door...

Almost to the bottom of the stairs, her face lit up as she saw her freedom. The door was only a few feet away. But, once again, a powerful force pushed her from behind. With a colossal scream she grabbed onto the bannister and caught herself before she tumbled below. Her feet dangled down the stairs, her wet sneakers sliding on the wood as she tried to stand up again. Then, just as it had before, the little door at the bottom opened. Lightning struck and brightened the interior as Taryn watched in astonishment.

Forgetting her fear for a moment she scrambled to her feet and crawled towards the door. Remembering her flashlight, she turned it back on and shone it inside. It was empty, but...

Giving Miss Dixie another chance Taryn aimed her at the small space and let her go. The image that came back was as suspected: a crumpled mass in trousers and a white shirt buttoned down the front. His hair was dark and matted with blood. But she also saw something else—a loose board sticking up near his feet.

The board was pushed down now, flattened. The room was empty. Trying not to think about the body that had once been there and the spiders that could very well be there *now*, Taryn crawled inside. Somewhere, off in the distance, she could hear pounding on the front door as someone cried, "Let us in, let us in!" The storm had picked up now. Glass ruptured somewhere upstairs, the house shook, and lightning cracked so close she was certain it would send all of them up in flames. She could faintly hear the sound of a woman screaming, piercing and helpless, and sobs that dug into her soul. Still, she continued crawling to the edge of the room, towards the floorboard.

Using her flashlight for leverage, she pulled at the board with all her might. It didn't budge. Again she tried to dislodge it. The force sent her sprawling backwards, causing her to hit her head on the wall behind her. "Damn it," she cried. Daniel was outside, calling her name, but he sounded a million miles away. She would give up, she had to. She couldn't do this.

"I can't do this," she screamed. "I need help."

As she crawled back towards the door, however, it slammed shut. Now she was alone in the tiny room. Unable to stand she crouched at the door and beat on it, calling for help. "You can't keep me in here!" she cried, panicked. "You can't!"

A whisper, so light she might have imagined it, came to her left ear. "Help me," it pleaded. "Help me."

"Oh for God's sake," she muttered, disgusted with herself. She was terrified but at least she still had her flashlight. The sooner she did this, the better.

Scuttling back over to the board, she dug at it again. This time it sprang loose. Part of her fingernail ripped off in the process and she swore aloud, partly in pain and partly in frustration. She'd done it, though; it was open. Peering into the dark hole she saw what she'd come for. Not just one bag, but many. "Jesus!" she laughed hysterically, her hands shaking. "Holy hell!"

Still unable to believe her eyes she reached into the dampness and pulled out a cloth bag, marveling at the weight in her hands. Laying the bag on the floor beside her, she tried again, pulled out another, and then another, and then her hand touched something else—a silver baby rattle. Hannah's? Her eyes stung a little through her happiness. But there was a name inscribed on it. Her flashlight illuminated it: Sally. Shrugging, Taryn laid it aside and continued to dig into the hole. The bags just kept coming. Sitting back on her heels she laughed and laughed, grime and dust coating her hands and face. "We did it," she shouted, looking at the mounds around her, the rattle sparkling even in the dark. "We did it!"

At that moment, the little door sprung open with ease and a face appeared before her.

Now, frantically, she wriggled towards it. Crying and laughing, she fell upon the figure and wrapped her arms around him.

"Matt," she cried. "Matt."

Chapter 20

Matt, Joe, Willow, Daniel, and Taryn sat at a table together in the small diner. They were waiting on their food, but none of them had much of an appetite; they were too excited.

"So how much in total?" Taryn asked with pleasure.

"We're not sure yet but they're thinking at least half a million dollars' worth," Willow replied, laying her hand on top of Daniel's. 'The price of gold is high these days."

"And the owners?" Matt asked.

"Over the moon. They don't know what to do with themselves. Of course, they won't sell to the developers now, especially since they learned the fire was started by one of their minions. Maybe the big guys knew about it, maybe it was a rogue thing, but either way they say they'd rather declare bankruptcy then see it go to a development. They're selling to us, seeing as to how they don't suffer from a cash shortage," Joe supplied.

"Ironically, since relaying the story on our campaign we've raised the money to buy it outright and start on the improvements," Daniel disclosed proudly. "More than $200,000."

Taryn sat back, shocked. "How did you manage that?"

"Well," Daniel shrugged. "People love the paranormal. Now it won't just be a museum. We're going to offer ghost hunting tours, psychic workshops, all kinds of things. We think it's going to be a paranormal center."

"The ghost business is good I guess," Matt muttered, casting a glance at Taryn.

She smiled back in return. She'd been unable to keep her name out of the local paper, or the ghost story aspect of what happened. Both Willow and Daniel had sworn to the press they saw a woman in a long red dress pacing back and forth across the foyer and then guarding the little room. "It's how we knew where you were," Willow explained. Once they'd seen the pictures, nothing had kept them quiet. Now Taryn's email and phone were blowing up from folks wanting her opinion on everything from unsolved disappearances to their sick pets.

"Can we look again?" Daniel pleaded.

Sighing, Taryn pulled out Miss Dixie and turned her on. The pictures of Permelia in her bedroom were one thing; she'd pored over those again and again, fascinated and terrified by Permelia's closeness and wanting. But she hadn't looked at the pictures taken in the guest room until the next morning. Those were something of another breed. In this room, her pictures had revealed something nobody was ready for, or expecting. Paneling in the walls covered an opening, a door that was open in her shots. Although it was difficult to see, unless you looked closely, an almost irrational and unbelievable image of an arm, leg, and slumped-over body was positioned inside the wall. Blood trailed from the door to the middle of the floor, the drops becoming fainter as they stretched out across the hardwood.

"So what do you think *really* happened there?" Willow asked.

They all looked at Taryn expectantly, as though she had all the answers. "Honestly? I'm not completely sure. But I think I have some ideas." She looked at Matt for support and he placed his hand comfortably on her knee.

"We think the first killing, the man she wrote about, was probably an accident. Or, at the very least, self-defense," he started. Taryn had already debriefed them on her dreams. They would never have solid evidence as far as that went, but nobody was questioning it as truth, not in light of what they'd discovered.

"They got his money and disposed of his body. I don't think anything happened after that, at least not for a long time," Taryn said. "We looked at the bank records the historical society had and they made a modest living for many years. Probably all the way up to James' death."

"With him gone, things got rough again," Matt continued. "Her family wouldn't take her back, there was a lot more competition here...Things just weren't in Permelia's favor."

"So she killed again?" Willow interjected.

Taryn nodded. "She was attacked. That had to have soured her against men. And then losing her child, her husband...Deserted by her dad. Let's face it, Permeliawas probably a little out of sorts. I'm sure she was confused. I think, at first, she hid the body in the wall. There were more than a dozen watches and bags in the hole. I'd say she killed at least that many people. Maybe more."

"Why the wall?" Daniel asked.

"She was a little woman. A body is deadweight," Matt explained. "It would've been hard for her to take it anywhere else. But a body starts to smell after a time. She couldn't have hidden it forever."

"So then we think she dragged them downstairs, kept them in the little room until it was time to get them to the sinkhole."

Daniel and Willow looked at one another and then both shook in mock horror at the same time. "But how did she get the bodies to the sinkhole? If they were so heavy?"

"I don't know," Taryn admitted. "Maybe a wagon. Maybe she paid someone off. But I imagine if you pulled a wagon right up to the porch it would be easy enough to get the body onto it. Then it's just a matter of kicking it into the hole when you got there."

"Or she could've chopped it up, piece by piece," Daniel suggested.

They all shuddered at the thought.

"You know, she sounds scary as hell but it's still hard to think of her as a murderer," Willow said after awhile. "I mean, I actually kind of admire her. I'm guessing she targeted single men, men with money and without any ties. They wouldn't be missed. She wasn't just killing at random, either. She was trying to survive."

"She killed more than a dozen people," Daniel exclaimed, taken a little aback at Willow's words.

"She was a woman in the 19th century who was trying to run a business. Nobody wanted her. She was turned away by her family. Her baby was dead. Her husband was dead.

She was just trying to survive the only way she thought she could. And look what she did! She kept the inn running and died a respected lady," Willow responded. "You have no idea how hard it is for women to be taken seriously, respected, even today."

"You mean the whole glass ceiling thing?" Daniel asked.

"The glass ceiling, less pay, sexual harassment, rape…" Willow let her words trail off. "She found a way to make it. Albeit, a morbid one."

Taryn nodded. She'd felt the same way about Delphina.

"You couldn't get in," she directed at Daniel. "When you knew I was in there."

"It was like the door and windows were nailed shut," he claimed. "Until Matt got there. And he walked right through it like it was nothing."

"I got your message and came straight from the airport. I knew something was happening. I could feel it. The closer I got, the stronger it was," he explained. "I thought…well, it doesn't matter what I thought. You're okay."

"I'm okay," she smiled and took his hand. "I'm okay."

"And there's something else," Willow added. She prodded Daniel with her thumb. "Tell her."

"Tell me what?" Taryn asked, confused.

"I guess I know something you don't," Daniel smirked with pride. "But you're going to love this."

Willow reached into her black leather purse and pulled out a Xeroxed sheet of paper. There was old fashioned handwriting on it and Taryn wasn't sure what it was. As she quickly read over it, however, her confusion only grew.

"What is this?" she asked at last, putting it down on the table.

"It's a deed," Willow supplied.

"I see that," she said. "So Permelia gave someone a house?"

"Property, to be exact," Daniel offered. "We're assuming the house was built later."

"Lydia and Paul..." Taryn mused, reading the names. "That's the couple who took care of the horses and did the cooking."

"And her friends," Daniel added.

"But there's one more thing," Willow smiled. "This might make things make more sense."

Reaching into her purse a second time, she pulled out another sheet of paper. This was a Xeroxed photograph, grimy and faded with age. The baby was around ten months old, chubby and smiling, as it did its best to hold still for the camera. At the bottom was the word "Sally."

"You don't think..." Taryn breathed.

"That's what we think," Daniel nodded. "We're thinking Permelia was pregnant when James died and, instead of raising the baby, gave her to her friends."

"Along with the house," Willow said. "Or land, as it may be."

"It's a stretch, a leap," Taryn mused.

"Maybe, maybe not," Daniel shrugged. "We called Miranda and talked to her. Records show that Paul went to work on the railroad about six months after James died. All those years of working for him and then he just quits? And his wife, too. Yet at the same time they get this land?"

"I think she was depressed, maybe guilty, and didn't know what to do," Willow said gently. "Remember in her letter to her sister she talked about making hard decisions? She gave her daughter to people she trusted, people who would take care of her. She couldn't take care of herself, much less a child. Maybe she'd already started killing. We just don't know."

"But the address," Taryn sputtered.

"I know," Willow smiled. "That wasn't lost on us, either. Do you think Delphina knew her great-grandmother was the town's most famous proprietress?"

"And murderer?" Daniel threw in.

Afterword

*T*aryn sank back into the soft pillows and sighed.

"Now *this* is fancy."

"I told you I aimed to please," Matt smiled. "I'm glad you came back to Florida with me."

"And I'm glad you bought a new couch. That futon had to go. And, besides, I'm not ready to be alone again. I've been alone for a long time."

"You're never alone, Taryn," he said adamantly, stroking his finger across her cheek. "Never."

"They're talking mental hospital for Delphina," she sighed. "Maybe because of her advanced age and maybe because nobody can believe that an old woman could actually do the things she did. At least, not one in her right mind."

"You kind of draw old, psychotic women don't you?" he teased.

She smiled. "I don't think Delphina was psychotic, though. Maybe a little misguided. I'm going to keep in touch with her. She helped me. I think she could use a friend about now. I have a feeling that small town isn't going to be generous to her."

317

"Do you feel like you finished this?"

Taryn considered his question before answering. "She wanted my help. Help to save the tavern? Help in understanding her? I think I did both to the best of my ability. But I also think *she* helped *me*."

They sat together in comfortable silence for a few minutes. Matt flipped through some paperwork in his briefcase while Taryn read a page in her Nora Roberts book three times before she realized it.

"I got another job," she professed at last. "It's different this time."

"Yeah, what is it?" He put down his papers and gave her his full attention.

"Teaching. In Georgia. They want me to come down to a community college and lead a month-long workshop on painting. Kind of a historical 'fill in the gaps' deal."

Matt raised his eyebrows. "That's different. How do you feel about that?"

"I don't know. It's what I do but I've never tried to teach before. The money is good. That burden has been lifted a little, okay a lot, but I still have to think about it."

"It sounds like something you might enjoy. Be a good change. Quiet."

"I know," she agreed. "Already I'm getting a ton of emails from people wanting me to come solve mysteries for them. And I don't want to be known as the woman with the magical camera. I enjoy painting, I enjoy my job."

"Everyone changes, Taryn. Maybe this is just a new phase," Matt suggested. "Something different."

"You know they've already got people wanting to come stay at Griffith Tavern and it's not even completed? They're already taking reservations."

"Like I said," he laughed, "the paranormal sells."

Stretching out, she laid her head in his lap. He stroked her hair, his fingertips brushing her ear.

"Tift Merrit's 'Bramble Rose,'" she mumbled.

"What?" Matt asked absently.

"Permelia, me, Delphina. Delphina said we all had skeletons. Okay, so she and Permelia had literal ones. But it's more than that. We were all women, intrinsically *good* women I think, who nobody knew. Maybe that's why I ultimately felt connected to them."

"I know you," he stated firmly, his hand coming to rest on her shoulder. "And I am here, no matter where you go next. Ghosts or not."

Special Notes

The people in this story are entirely fictional. However, there are a few things that inspired the actual story, although I took a great amount of liberty with the actual details.

There actually was a Griffith Tavern. It was located between Georgetown and Cynthiana in Kentucky. I saw it in person several times. By the time I discovered it, it was in poor condition. Unfortunately, it has since been torn down. I do not know its story. I simply borrowed its name and some details of its exterior (I was never inside).

Stage coach inns, of course, are real. I did extensive research on them before writing the story. Many contained both taverns and inns which is what I made Griffith Tavern out to be.

The inspiration for the actual story came from two places. When I was a child my mom and I drove to Indianapolis to visit family one Christmas. It was cold and snowy and we got down to a snail's pace on the interstate. Bored, and a little scared of the bad weather, I asked my mom to tell me a story. I liked it when she made one up on the spot. From the interstate we could see several

320

farmhouses off in the distance. They all had their lights on and looked inviting. So, my mom started making up this story about us getting stranded on the interstate, walking to one of the farmhouses, and seeking shelter. The story took a turn in a different direction when our new hosts poisoned our hot chocolate and locked us in a bedroom. Next door, we could hear people scratching on the walls. They were also locked in their room.

That was the seed for the main part of this story. However, a second story kind of finished it out. While doing research on *Haunted Estill County* several people told me about a woman who used to take in oil workers as boarders. She apparently killed some of her boarders and threw their bodies in a sinkhole. Later, another person told me that wasn't the real story, that the woman had an affair with a slave and when her husband came back and found a mixed racial child HE turned and killed the man and the woman. Still, the sinkhole story stayed with me.

Special Thanks

Of course, I have to thank my mother for this story. Without her input it wouldn't have been possible. I'd also like to thank Tammy Rose for telling me the first story about the boarding house woman and the sinkhole.

There were many people along the way who offered a lot of encouragement. Steve Young of Pickers Paradise in Irvine, Kentucky and his wife Connie are not only some of the nicest people I've met but are also extremely supportive. They've held a book signing for me and continue to keep my books in stock.

I received lots of support online in the writing of this story. Some of those folks include: Carrie Shields, Lauren McCord, Mandy Reichert, Cheryl McHauer, Tori VG, Carla Tenorio, and Rebecca Powell.

Special thanks also go out to Anne and Fletcher Gabbard. Without them and their hospitality, I couldn't have finished this book.

As always, I have to thank Ashley Kirk and the late Jim. There's nothing the three of us liked doing better than driving around and finding old houses to explore. One of my fondest memories is of being pregnant with my first child and Jim and I trying to figure out if we could hoist me in

322

through a window of an abandoned mansion without hurting
anything.

Sneak Peek at *Dark Hollow Road*: Book 3 in Taryn's Camera

As the radio blared George Strait's "Check Yes Or No" Cheyenne stood in front of the full-length mirror, gazing at herself as she adjusted her tank top and shorts. She was glad she'd used the self-tanner from Bath & Body Works, even if it did make her a little orange. Orange was better than white. She needed to get to the tanning bed, and soon. She'd already straightened her hair and now it hung down to her waist in a long sheet of molasses, not like the frizzy mess it usually was. Her eyes, encircled with liner and dazzling with glitter eye shadow from Maybelline, stood out from her pale face. Still watching herself, she sat down on the laminate bedroom floor amidst the rejected piles of clothes and tugged on her red leather cowboy boots, a Christmas present from last year. She continue to hum with the radio as the song changed from George to Jason Aldean.

School was out—for good, too. With graduation being three days ago this would be her first official weekend as a free woman. Sure, college was starting in the fall but that was months away. She had the whole summer to hang out, enjoy herself, not have to listen to anyone's rules. She didn't even have to go to college in the fall if she wanted; she could take some time off and just earn herself some money. She'd thought about that.

But tonight...tonight was what mattered.

There were three hundred people in Cheyenne's high school and every one of them would be at Chris Hinkle's party. Or, at least, everyone who *mattered*. Like Evan. Nobody cared what they did out on that farm. Some of the kids were even talking about skinny dipping, even though the creek would be freezing. Then there was the booze. She had free clearance to stay out all night, if she wanted to. She didn't even have *that* at prom. But she was an adult now. Today was her birthday and eighteen couldn't have fallen at a better time.

A gaggle of giggles echoed down the hall and soon the bedroom door was filled with a handful of teenage girls, each one prettier and younger than the other. "Have you seen my straightener?" Krissy, a leggy redhead, demanded with a pout.

"It's in the bathroom," Cheyenne said absently. She stood up, turned around, and looked at her backside in the mirror again. It was important to make sure you looked good from all angles. She was almost ready. Being May, it was still a little too cool for her top so she grabbed a jacket, just in case. Her blood was pumping, the anticipation of the night almost more than she could take.

In just about half an hour she'd be sipping on a Bud, dancing around the bonfire, talking to Evan. In just about half an hour she'd be starting her brand new life.

And, by the end of the night, she'd be dead.

About the Author

Rebecca Patrick-Howard is the author of several books including the first book in her paranormal mystery trilogy *Windwood Farm*. She lives in eastern Kentucky with her husband and two children.

Visit her website at www.rebeccaphoward.net and sign up for her newsletter to receive free books, special offers, and news.

<u>Taryn's Camera Series</u>
Windwood Farm
Griffith Tavern
Dark Hollow Road
Shaker Town
Jekyll Island
Taryn's Pictures: Photos from Taryn's Camera

<u>True Hauntings</u>
Haunted Estill County
More Tales from Haunted Estill County
A Summer of Fear
The Maple House
Four Months of Terror

Two Weeks: A True Haunting

Three True Tales of Terror

Other Books

Coping with Grief: The Anti-Guide to Infant Loss

Three Minus Zero

Estill County in Photos

Haunted: Ghost Children Stories from Beyond

Visit her website at www.rebeccaphoward.net to sign up for her newsletter to receive free books, special offers, and news.

Copyright

Visit Rebecca's website at www.rebeccaphoward.net to sign up for her newsletter to receive free books, special offers, and news.

https://www.facebook.com/rebeccahowardwrites

Rphwrites@yahoo.com

27779828R00187

Made in the USA
San Bernardino, CA
16 December 2015